The Empty Chair

Also by Edna Taylor and published by Ginninderra Press
The Skeleton in the Cupboard
Brief Encounters
The Attic

Edna Taylor

The Empty Chair

& other stories

The Empty Chair & other stories
ISBN 978 1 76041 675 1
Copyright © text Edna Taylor 2019
Cover: EVG Photos via StockSnap

First published 2019 by
GINNINDERRA PRESS
PO Box 3461 Port Adelaide 5015
www.ginninderrapress.com.au

Contents

The Experiment

Lucinda Langley was sitting in the corner of the art gallery. A slight, nondescript middle-aged lady with greying hair, wearing a beigey/brown outfit almost the same colour as the chair she was sitting on. No one was paying much attention to her, which was exactly the way she liked it.

She was watching people who were inspecting the paintings on display and taking mental notes of the various remarks as they passed judgement and made – in their opinion – profound observations on the pictures, which were, in Lucinda's opinion, absolutely ghastly, including her own, which was hanging up directly in front of her.

The paintings in this exhibition were called Modern Abstracts. Some were painted in strong primary colours, some in harmonising tones which had – also in Lucinda's opinion – no focus point and no message. Yet they were being admired. Hidden meanings were perceived, ambience was discussed, perfect balance and harmony were oohed and aahed over.

There was nothing under a thousand dollars, which made it all the more puzzling for Lucinda. She certainly wouldn't want any of them hanging on her wall. She had always painted landscapes in the rich warm colours of the outback, gumtrees, and pioneer cottages with a history that told a story.

Lucinda had had her paintings in this gallery for about five years now, on consignment. The gallery kept twenty-five per cent of the selling price. In the beginning she had sold well and even received commissions, but gradually things had changed. And after the last three months turn around when she could swap pictures over, there had been no sales. In fact, there had been no sales for the past six months.

'I'm so sorry, Lucinda.' Jan the gallery owner was apologetic. 'People don't seem to want traditional landscapes any more,' she sighed. 'It's such a pity. Your work is so beautiful.'

So Lucinda had taken the four unsold paintings home and this time hadn't swapped any over. Then she sat down and had a big think. She decided to do an experiment.

She regarded a big canvas board on the easel on which she had been planning to do an outback scene, and had already done some preliminary drawings. Suddenly coming to a decision, she rubbed away all the sketches, cleaned up the canvas and then gathered up all her tubes of acrylic paint. She usually painted in oils, but decided not to waste them this time in case things didn't work out.

Lucinda squeezed all the red, white and blue colours onto her palate; she found some black and squeezed that out too.

This was all completely out of her comfort zone. No planning, no careful drawing, no attention to perspective. She just dipped her biggest brush into some water and then into two of the colours. Then, holding her breath, she stood back a little from the easel and flicked the paint, gently at first, and there were just a few dribbles falling down the canvas. So she tried harder. Great globs of paint stuck to the board. Some dribbled down and some melded into other paint. She took some more paint and started to do great swirls and slashes among all the rest.

In fact, Lucinda started to get quite carried away. She was suddenly feeling exhilarated and more liberated than she had ever felt in her life. She stopped for a moment and stood well back to take stock. She looked amazed at the glorious mess. Indeed, for Lucinda this was a rather overwhelming experience. She couldn't believe she had actually painted this monstrosity, although she reluctantly had to admit that perhaps she had actually enjoyed herself.

So she sat down and had a cup of tea and another big think.

One thing was for sure: she couldn't possibly put her name on it. She doodled on her shopping list pad for a bit, then wrote the name Perry Mentle. This was indeed a big experiment on her part and therefore quite apt, she thought. So without thinking any further about it, she carefully wrote her new name and the date on the corner of the picture.

Lucinda couldn't believe that she was actually thinking about offering it for the upcoming yearly exhibition at the gallery. It went against every thing the artist in her soul could contemplate, but nothing ventured, nothing gained, she told herself. She didn't even put a frame around it. There was no way she would go that far, she had decided. It wasn't worth it.

Jan had been totally surprised when she had brought the painting into the gallery. 'Wow, Lucinda,' she had exclaimed, 'this is so – um - different.' She had regarded her in awe. 'Who would've thought? Well, we'll see,' she added. 'You never know!' She had given Lucinda a little hug. 'Best of luck, but I've got to warn you, we have some excellent work in this time.'

So that was why she was now sitting in the gallery, nervously, it must be said, watching the people, listening to their observations of her painting, which she had called *Black Swans at Sunset*. She had laughed as she wrote the name on the on the description tag pasted up on the wall alongside the picture.

She had also daringly put the price at one thousand five hundred dollars. Nobody in their right mind would buy it, she thought, then leaned forward as she caught the words from a woman who, with her husband or whoever, had been looking at her painting for a few minutes.

'Absolutely beautiful,' she was gushing. 'That would go so well in the lounge room, and that shade of blue would match exactly the blue in my new cushion covers. It's so imaginative,' she continued. 'I can even see the black swans. Do you like it darling?' She implored him, 'Please may we get it?'

Lucinda was transfixed as she watched the man nod, 'Sure, OK, if you like it that much,' and they headed off to find Jan, who happily put a red Sold sticker on the corner of the painting.

She spotted Lucinda sitting unobtrusively in her corner and gave her a wink and a wave.

Lucinda almost burst out laughing as she left the gallery. On the way home, she stopped at the shopping centre and bought two of the biggest canvases she could find, some more paint and an apron. She had splattered herself a fair bit before; she would need something to cover up.

Lucinda regarded her beautiful landscapes stacked up against the wall. Maybe one day tastes would turn around again and she would be ready. In the meanwhile, she would try to banish the word 'traitor' from her mind as she began planning another onslaught onto a fresh canvas.

Of Chalk and Cheese

Robin Goodfellow had been teaching history at the same school for thirty years and today he was giving his last lesson. Tomorrow he would be retired. He wasn't sure how he felt about that and what he was going to do with himself. He would miss the children and he thought they would probably miss him. But it was time.

The students called him Chalky because he still used chalk on a blackboard instead of a marker pen on a whiteboard – and maybe because of his chalk-white beard – but he didn't mind.

He was old-fashioned, he would be the first to admit it. His classroom was the only one in the school that still had a blackboard. He was allowed this concession by the school board because (a) he had requested it and (b) his students all got high marks and gave him respect, which was more than some of the younger teachers managed to achieve. Although that, he thought, probably had nothing to do with the blackboard.

He had been talking about the history of paper, and how children in the olden days had to use slate boards and chalk. They were slightly interested when he told them about how the Chinese invented it and he had written 'CHINA' on the blackboard. He turned around as someone called out, 'Sir?'

Someone had shot up a hand.

'But why do we need to know about this?' the boy asked. 'We don't even hardly need to use paper.' He indicated his laptop. 'It's all on this.'

'We still have to print it out,' someone else said, 'when we have to do homework.'

And so it went. He encouraged open debate and liked listening to their thoughts and opinions. Robin let them go on, without interrupting, until it was silent again. They looked at him expectantly.

He usually had plenty to say when someone disputed or raised questions about his history lessons and he always came up with reason and logic as to why it was important. Why history was important. He always researched his subject and generally had answers ready for the questions he knew they would throw at him. He also knew that if they were really interested they could look it up on the net and that, if they were not, then no amount of lecturing would make any difference.

Today he said nothing. He looked around his class for a moment, his eyes resting briefly on each boy. He glanced at his watch. 'Off you go then,' he said, 'it's time for lunch,' just as the bell sounded.

'What about homework, sir?' someone asked. 'To do over the break.'

'There'll be no homework this time.' he said.

They went quietly, sensing something was amiss, but not knowing. He hadn't told them that this was to be his last day. He didn't want a fuss. He had enjoyed his class this term. There were a few boys who he thought would do really well in the future.

Robin sighed as he acknowledged the truth to himself. He hadn't caught up with all the new technology and didn't understand much of it. It was just as well he was going now and let some eager young person who liked to use a whiteboard try and teach history to these tech-savvy teenagers.

The classroom had emptied and it was quiet now as he opened the top drawer of his desk. Next to his box of chalk was a blue plastic box containing his lunch. He unwrapped a roll filled with a large slab of cheese resting on a bed of Vegemite. He preferred to eat in his classroom instead of the staffroom, where it was noisy with chatter and filled with people he hardly knew. They came and left again so quickly these days. There weren't many of the old-timers left and he had nothing in common with the young ones. The old adage about chalk and cheese crossed his mind, and he smiled as he bit into his roll.

Robin was lost in thought when one of the new younger staffers gave a brief knock on the door and then came into the room. He looked up enquiringly.

'You're wanted in the staff room, Mr Goodfellow,' she said.

'What for?' he asked

'I don't know,' she smiled. 'I was just asked to come and get you.'

He wrapped up his half eaten roll and put it back in the box. He'd finish it later.

When he got to the staffroom, he was surprised to see all of the teachers there, and he stopped by the door. Something's afoot, he thought, and watched Bill Harden the principal as he stepped towards him and started clapping. Then they all joined in and Robin looked around with a dazed expression until he realised they were all applauding him.

He didn't want this. He didn't want a fuss. He needed to leave quietly. Nevertheless, he smiled and shook hands with people who wished him well in his retirement and he listened to the thanks and praise for his contribution to the school for so many years.

Then he was presented with a laptop computer.

'Now you'll have to learn how to use it, Chalky,' one wag remarked, and they all laughed.

He gave a reply and thanked them, but afterwards couldn't remember what he'd said, it was all a bit of a blur.

The lunch break was soon over. Some people had classes to go to but most of the students were having sports out on the oval for the last afternoon of term and so goodbyes were called and everyone departed. Robin went back to his empty classroom, unwrapped his cheese roll, finished it off then took a swig from his water bottle to wash it down.

He went over to the blackboard and erased all the writing. They'll probably put this straight into the storeroom, he thought.

Then Robin Goodfellow went out to the car park, carefully balancing his new laptop on top of the cardboard box containing his personal stuff and his box of chalk.

Then he drove home.

Halloween

'Can I have that one, please?' Peter was pointing towards a particularly ugly Halloween mask on the shop's display counter.

Patty frowned. 'That's horrible, Peter.' She turned to the shop assistant. 'Have you got any others?' she asked him.

'Sorry, ma'am, that's all that's left. The rest are all sold out.' What he didn't tell her was that he had bought a cheap job lot of masks, which were supposed to be a variety but had turned out to be all the same. Consequently, most of the kids had the same masks, except those who had saved them from last year.

Patty had no option but to buy it. Peter however was rapt. Halloween on 31 October was also his eighth birthday, and so this year for the first time, Patty decided that he could have a few friends over for a birthday party, and very reluctantly agreed, after constant pleas from Peter, that they could all go trick or treating afterwards. 'Just around the local neighbourhood,' she told him, 'and provided the other parents agree and help with supervising the children.'

So it was arranged. Seven of his friends enjoyed a great birthday party, devoured the birthday cake and ice cream, tried on their masks and then with much excitement started out with their trick and treating. It was getting dusk by the time they were all organised, streets were allocated, and warnings were given about never going inside a house even if they knew the person.

Four mums were each allocated two children to supervise. They were all familiar with the area and most of the householders were ready for the expected onslaught and had bags of goodies ready. There were a couple of people who didn't believe in handing out lollies, but were happy to do some tricks, like old Mr Tanner, who did some juggling with oranges and then handed them out to the children, and another couple who sang some nursery rhymes.

All in all, it was a good fun evening, with everyone entering into the spirit of Halloween. They had all agreed to meet at the end of the road before starting down the other side. It was getting darker now and the ugly masks were showing an eerie greenish glow. They were of course all identical and, in Patty's opinion, totally gruesome.

She counted the children, a force of habit since her job as teacher's aide, when it became necessary every time they took children anywhere. She counted nine. Patty frowned and started again. Maybe she had counted someone twice, but before she had finished they had all started walking again, so she grabbed Peter's hand and followed the others.

They had just about reached the other end of the street when Patty's phone rang. It was Bob, her husband, wanting to know when they would be getting home.

'Just about done,' she said. 'We'll be home soon.' She looked for Peter, who had momentarily disappeared, and called him. 'Come on, Peter. We're going home now.'

The street lights had begun to glow. Everyone was saying their goodbyes, and agreeing how much fun it had been.

Patty grabbed hold of Peter's arm and propelled him towards the car park. 'Don't keep disappearing, Peter,' she told him. 'I told you to stay with me.'

She was dropping Meg, her friend, and her two boys off at their home first, and the three boys jumped into the back of the car. Quiet now, still excited, but tired and busy with their bags of lollies.

'Thanks, Patty,' Meg called as they got out of the car. 'See you later."

Bob opened the front door as they pulled into the driveway, and after they got inside, Patty turned to her son. 'You can take your mask off, Peter,' she said and held out her hand. 'And I think perhaps I'll look after those lollies for now. You've had enough for today.'

The boy hesitated for a moment and Patty took a closer look at his clean white T-shirt. How had he managed to keep it so clean? It was then that she noticed his hair. It looked lighter. It didn't look like Peter's hair.

Her heart started thudding as she repeated with a wavering voice, 'Peter, take off that mask.'

Slowly he removed it and she couldn't speak. She stared, aghast.

'Who are you?' she managed then. 'And where's Peter? Bob!' she shouted, hysteria creeping into her voice. 'Bob!'

The boy looked up at her, his slightly lopsided smile hauntingly familiar, as was the little dimple in his right cheek. He looked searchingly at her, a strange look of familiarity and seeming remembrance shone for a brief moment in the depth of very blue eyes, then he turned and ran out of the still open front door.

Patty was so shocked she couldn't move for a moment. Then, coming to her senses, she hurried outside and ran down the path to the road She looked both ways but there was no one there.

Bob appeared behind her. 'What's wrong, Patty. You sounded a bit hysterical. I was in the garage,' he added.

'It wasn't Peter,' she said. 'It was someone else.'

'What do you mean, it wasn't Peter? Where's Peter?' He looked at her accusingly.'

Patty went back inside sat down on a kitchen chair and started to cry. 'It wasn't Peter. It was another boy who looked like Peter. He even had his dimple, but it wasn't him. I thought it was Peter,' she was shaking and making no sense.

Bob looked at her in amazement. 'You mean to tell me you brought someone else's kid home, and you didn't notice?' He was starting to sound frantic. 'So where's Peter then?'

His phone rang before she could say anything and, angry now, he shouted, 'Yes, what?' Then his voice quietened. 'Thanks, Julie,' he said and then listened for a moment or two before saying, 'I'll be there in ten minutes,' before putting the phone down.

Patty looked up 'What is it, Bob? Who was that?'

'It was Julia Parks,' he told her. 'She has Peter. You apparently left him behind and took another boy home, but she didn't know who it could have been because everyone else was accounted for.' His voice softened. 'Look, it's OK, Patty. Peter's safe. I'll go and pick him up.' He kissed her lightly on her cheek. 'I'll be back soon, then we'll talk about it. By the way,' he added, 'Julie asked if you'd found a mask. Her youngest dropped it and it got lost.'

Patty had composed herself by the time they returned. Peter was laughing and had taken the awful mask off. Patty thought that his father must have explained what had happened and Peter thought it was all a great joke.

Bob came into the house. He looked at her, his eyes puzzled, 'Come out here for a minute,' he said, and they both followed him to the veranda alongside the front porch.

The outside light was on, illuminating a small table and two chairs. 'Look,' Bob pointed.

On the table there was a Halloween mask and, alongside, someone had neatly arranged some jelly snakes in the shape of the name Paul.

'Did you do that, Peter?' Patty asked him now, knowing that he couldn't have.

'No, not me,' he said, whooping with glee as he scooped up the snakes. 'He knows they're my favourites. He must have left them for me,' and he ran inside.

Patty stared after him, wonder in her eyes. They had told their son about Paul, his twin who had died when barely three months old. Sometimes she had heard Peter talking to himself, when alone in his room. She had thought perhaps he had an imaginary friend, as was common among children with no siblings. But she never questioned it. He was a happy well adjusted child, so she didn't worry too much,

The grief had never left her, though, and the anger at the fatal heart problem that had taken her baby son.

Patty and Bob sat down, both with thoughts that didn't make sense. Thinking about Paul. Patty knew what Bob was thinking with his very logical and commsense approach to life.

'Coincidence, that's all it is,' she heard him say. 'There has to be a reasonable explanation. Some homeless kid maybe.'

But Patty's heart was overriding what her head was telling her and she suddenly felt an overwhelming sense of peace, and of an acceptance without understanding. And it was all right.

She smiled. 'Peter,' she called. 'It's time you were getting ready for bed.'

Mangrove Flats

One

Jenny put her brush in the jar of turps, wiped her hands on her apron, then stood up and stretched. She had been busily painting for an hour or so, and it was time to step back and study her picture. She frowned and squinted. Something was off; she wasn't sure what. She decided to go and get a coffee before having another look to see if it was worth pursuing.

Cup in hand, Jenny sauntered around the class, looking over the other students' work, They were encouraged to review one another's paintings, 'to get a another perspective on things', their tutor Marie told them. Everyone was painting something different and Jenny stopped by Simon, who was sketching a landscape with an old farmhouse as the main subject.

'Hi, Jen, how are you going?' He liked Jenny and was pleased she had stopped to chat.

'That looks great, Simon,' she said, admiring his work. She looked closer and then picked up a photograph he was using as a reference. She stood very still as she suddenly felt a chill pass through her. She shivered and studied the photo more closely.

'Jenny? What's up?' Simon had noticed the intense way she was studying the picture. He put down his brush.

'Simon, where did you get this picture?' she asked him now.

'Er…well.' He thought for a moment. 'It was one of a bunch I got which belonged to an old family friend. He died recently and Jill – his wife – sent me a heap of his photos. He used to have a thing about old houses. She knew I was into painting and sent them on to me to use for reference. Why? What's wrong, Jenny?'

'I don't know It's just…I recognise this house.'

'You do?'

'I'm sure of it. Where was it taken – do you know?' She handed the picture back to him.

Simon turned it over. There was something written there. The writing was very faint and hard to read.

Jenny leaned forward, 'What does it say?'

Simon peered closely. 'It just says "old house at Mangrove Flats". I've never heard of the place. Have you?' he asked her.

Jenny shook her head. 'No, I don't think so.'

'Well,' he smiled, 'if you recognise it, you must have been there.'

'Yes, I suppose – but there again, there must be plenty of old houses look like this except –' Jenny pointed to the photo '– I remember this windmill at the back, and the stone walls and the chimney. See? And,' she almost whispered, 'it gives me a really bad feeling.'

Simon glanced up at her and saw that she was genuinely disturbed. 'Well,' he said, 'I'll tell you what. I'll try and Google it tonight and have a look at some maps to see it I can find this Mangrove Flats place. And then I'll let you know when we come to class next week.'

'No – no, Simon, there's something about that house that makes me feel – I don't know – strange. I can't explain. But I need to find out. Simon?'

'Yes?'

'Would you mind giving me a call if you discover anything? I've got South Australian maps, but I don't think it's anywhere near Adelaide. I think I'd know. I'll write down my phone number for you.'

'I've got a better idea.' Simon was sounding enthusiastic. 'How about I meet you for lunch tomorrow and we'll see what I've come up with. If it's that important to you, that is.'

Jenny was suddenly looking very uncertain. 'Lunch? Well, I don't know, I suppose – are you sure?'

'Sure? Sure about what? Looking up my maps or asking you to lunch,' he grinned mischievously.

'Well, both sort of. I mean – well, OK, that's very kind of you, Simon.'

'Kind? No, Jenny, really. It's Saturday tomorrow, right?'

'Er…right.'

'And you don't work tomorrow, right?'

'No.'

'So there you go! Lunch it is. What about Chinese. D'you like Chinese?'

'Er…yes.'

'Great! Shall I pick you up…?'

Jenny shook her head. 'No, oh no no, Simon, I'll meet you somewhere.' She was feeling quite flustered and a little overwhelmed. Making quick decisions wasn't a strong point with Jenny. She liked to think about things first.

'OK. Well how about that place next to the Town Hall. Foo Chens at 12.30?'

Jenny hesitated for a long moment while Simon waited. 'Yes, all right then,' she said and quickly turned back to her painting table before she could change her mind.

Simon was had a big grin on his face as he started cleaning his brushes. 'See you tomorrow then, Jenny,' he called softly.

Two

That night, Jenny had a nightmare She was running away from somebody. She was out in the bush, running, running through sand. It was deep and her feet sank deeper with every step. She was terrified and she could hear someone behind her coming closer and closer. Then she tripped, and as she fell, saw a large hand reaching for her and she screamed…

She jerked awake and realised someone was shaking her. Jenny struggled to open her eyes and encountered Judy her housemate's concerned face.

'Jen, Jen, wake up,' she was saying. 'Wake up!'

Jenny blinked and slowly became aware of her surroundings. 'What's the matter, Jude?' She was struggling to remember.

'You were making such a racket I came to see what was wrong.' She studied her friend's face. 'Are you OK, Jen? It must have been a really nasty dream or something. You were yelling.'

'Was I? Yes, I guess it was.' Jenny looked at the bedclothes piled in a heap and realised she was soaked with sweat. 'Sorry, Jude,' she said. She still felt trembly. 'It must have been a nightmare. I haven't had one of those for years.' She pushed back her hair, which had stuck to her face. 'What time is it?'

'Still pretty early. I'm going back to bed for a bit, if you're sure you're all right?'

Jenny nodded. 'I'm good, thanks, Jude. I think I'll go for a shower,' she smiled, 'clear the cobwebs.'

The dream had all but disappeared by the time she had showered, tidied up and sat down for an early breakfast. She had to think about her date with Simon.

'So what's he like then? This Simon of yours?' Judy was asking later on that morning,

'I told you, he's not my Simon. He's just one of the art students.' She was peering at herself in the mirror. 'Do you think this will be all right? It is only lunch after all. It's not like it's a dinner date or anything.'

'You look fine. Stop worrying. In fact, that top looks brilliant with your red hair. Those autumn colours really suit you, Jen.' She gave her friend a little hug. 'You just go and enjoy yourself. Right?'

In fact, Jenny was feeling quite apprehensive. This was the first time in a very long while that she had actually been on a date. It was Judy who had nagged her about going out more, why she had joined the art club. To meet like-minded people. She liked to paint and was enjoying the class, learning a lot, and had indeed met some interesting people. Simon was probably the only one nearest to her age, around thirty, she guessed; the others were much older but so friendly that Jenny had lost all her earlier nervousness and was fitting in really well, plus the praise and encouragement from Marie had boosted her confidence immensely.

Luckily there was a bus stop close by the apartment, which made it easier to go to town without taking the car and battle for a car park. Jenny arrived early and found the restaurant without any problems. Her heart jumped a bit when she saw Simon waiting outside. He had a big smile as she approached, and held out his hand in greeting.

'Hi, Jenny,'

'Hi, Simon.'

They shook hands formally.

'You look nice,' Simon remarked. He was gazing at her approvingly and Jenny felt a blush coming on as he indicated the door. 'Are you right? Shall we go in?'

She nodded her thanks as he held the door for her. He had booked a table and they were seated fairly quickly. By the time they had studied the menu, had a drink in front of them and given their order for the meal, any awkwardness had disappeared.

'Well, did you find out anything, Simon? Is there such a place?' Jenny was looking anxious and then leaned over to look as he fished a map out of his pocket and spread it out over the table.

'Well, yes and no. It looks as though there used to be a place called Mangrove Flats, about eighty kilometres north, away on the coast. A small place with just a few old fishermen's shacks. It's not on any map, but I found it in a link on the net after investigating everything I could find to do with mangroves, It seems that the name was changed when Mangrove Flats became part of Berriwell, which is on the map. Here.' He put his finger on a remote-looking place, well away from the main road. 'There's a small population there, plus a police station and a pub.'

Simon leaned back in his chair, looking very pleased with himself, while Jenny could only gaze with approval as she realised how much effort he had put into the research.

'That's amazing, Simon. Thank you so much.' Jenny beamed with delight, then frowned. 'But I still can't remember Mangrove Flats. Perhaps,' she continued, 'I never knew it by name, just the house, but I don't know why.'

Then their lunch arrived and conversation stopped for a while.

'This looks awesome,' Jenny couldn't help remarking as they tucked into the chicken.

Simon was silent for a bit then, seemingly coming to a decision, put down his fork and regarded Jenny seriously. 'How would you feel, Jenny, if I offered to drive you over there, to Berriwell and see if we can find the old place? It'd only take an hour or so, and then we could stop somewhere for lunch,' he added. Simon waited while she pondered.

She could very well drive herself, she thought, but there again she was feeling so unsettled about the whole thing it would be nice to have some company. But she didn't really know Simon very well, did she, and now she had to make another decision. Jenny looked up at him, still undecided, but saw nothing but friendly concern in his eyes.

Then she surprised herself. 'OK,' she said, 'thanks, Simon, that's nice of you to offer.' Decision made, she thought. 'So when would be a good time to go?' she asked him now, feeling a little excited. This was so outside her comfort zone it all seemed a little surreal.

Simon wasn't about to waste time. 'What about tomorrow then?' he asked her.

So the arrangements were made. Jenny gave him her address and he was to pick her up at 9.30 the next morning.

Three

It was a bright spring day and, as they travelled north and left the suburbs behind, the landscape changed into farmland and vineyards. The countryside looked beautiful and Jenny relaxed as they chatted.

Simon asked about her family and she found herself telling him how she had been adopted when she was five years old. How her mother had disappeared, and she had been found lost and apparently abandoned. How the family had moved from Adelaide to Perth when she was still in primary school, and she had lived there ever since, until coming to Adelaide a year ago to share an apartment with Judy, her friend from high school. Judy had moved to Adelaide and had a job in the city and persuaded Jenny to come and join her. There had been a vacancy in the solicitor's office where she worked and Jenny now loved the place.

She hadn't talked about her childhood with anyone for a long time. Judy was the only one who knew what had happened apart from her parents. The nightmares she suffered as a child gradually went away, memories of the horror she had endured had been pushed to the back of her mind. The past was never spoken of and her adoptive parents were loving and kind. They had given her a good home and education.

But now, since seeing that picture of the old cottage, it seemed as though the nightmares had started again. As she related her story, Simon had listened with disbelief at first, and then he felt a great pity for the trauma she must have suffered as a child.

'So the police never got to the bottom of it?' he asked her. 'They never found your mum?'

She shook her head. 'No, but now I think it must have something to do with that cottage and Mangrove Flats,' she said, trying to sound matter-of-fact.

She didn't want to fall to pieces in front of Simon, but when he reached over and squeezed her hand and said, 'Don't worry, Jen, I'll help you get to the bottom of it all. Maybe we'll find some answers here,' she nearly lost it.

'Thanks,' was all she could manage, then pointed. 'Look, there's a roadhouse. How about we stop for a coffee?'

'Good idea.' Simon pulled in and over a drink they studied the map. 'I reckon it's about another ten ks,' he said, as they returned to the car, and then they were on their way again.

It wasn't long before there was a cross roads and a sign. 'Berriwell 6' it said, so they turned off the main highway onto a smaller road leading west, towards the coast. There were greenhouses, small farms and vegetable gardens each side and a few homes dotted about, then there was a WELCOME TO BERRIWELL sign.

It was a small town, and they cruised around checking everything out. There was a main street, with the usual few shops, a service station, bakery, general store and so on. They saw the pub and the police station, two churches and, surprisingly, an oval where some children were kicking a football around.

'Looks like a nice little town,' remarked Simon. He had stopped outside the petrol station. 'I'll go and fill up the tank, and see if anyone here has heard of Mangrove Flats.' Simon was getting out of the car.

'Please, Simon,' Jenny was looking for her purse, 'let me get the petrol.'

Simon shook his head, 'No, it's fine,' he said. He didn't want this to be an issue. 'Tell you what,' he added, 'you can treat me to lunch.'

Jenny nodded. 'That's a deal.'

He came back a few minutes later, holding the photograph of the cottage. He was smiling as he strapped himself back in the car.

'Well?' Jenny asked anxiously.

Simon handed her the picture. 'Here, hang onto this. We have to find the police station. The guy in the garage is fairly new and couldn't help, but he said that the local copper has been here for ever and knows everything about the place.'

It didn't take long to locate the police station and Inspector Sam Jamieson regarded the young couple with interest. He had been the local copper at Berriwell for the past thirty years, and was well liked and respected. He kept a tidy, mostly crime-free town and, although was nearing retirement, he still kept on top of things. Sam listened to Simon and then to Jenny as she related her story and then showed him the picture.

'So, do you recognise it?' she asked him, 'and is Mangrove Flats an actual place around here?'

Sam's weathered countenance creased into a frown as he studied the photo. He was quiet for a moment as he regarded the two anxious faces waiting for his response. He didn't answer straight away. Instead he looked closely at Jenny. 'What did you say your name was again?' he asked her.

'Jenny Martin,'

'Well, I'll be…!' Sam looked totally thunderstruck. 'You're little Jenny. It's you, isn't it? You've still got your lovely red hair.'

Jenny grabbed hold of Simon's hand. She was suddenly feeling very unsteady. 'You mean, you know me?'

'Know you?' he gave a great booming laugh. 'I was the one who took you in and my wife looked after you along with our kids until the social services came and took you away. I kept track of you after that. You went to a couple of foster homes, and then I found out you had been adopted by the Martins and went to live in Perth.' He looked a little sad. 'I never stopped worrying about you, and wondering what had really happened.' Sam still looked stunned. 'I can't believe it. Fancy you turning up again after all this time. It must be, let's see, twenty-five years ago, in '92.' He regarded Jenny's face, which was about to crumple up. 'This is all a bit too much for you, isn't it?' he said kindly.

'Are you sure it's me?' Jenny was having trouble talking.

'Ninety-nine per cent sure.' Then he smiled and knocked his head. 'Just remembered something. A birthmark like a heart, on your right leg near the ankle.'

Without a word, she bent down and lifted the bottom of her jeans. There it was, faint but still clear. There was no doubt any more.

'Here, sit yourselves down over here and I'll go and rustle up some coffee, then we'll have a chat.' Sam led them to the back of the office, where there was a table and some chairs, then disappeared.

'Are you OK?' Simon thought Jenny was about to faint, she looked so pale.

'I'll be fine in a minute,' she said. 'It's just, you know, the shock. Fancy him remembering after all this time.'

Sam was back shortly with a tray carrying coffees and some sugar. He put them on the table along with some spoons and a packet of biscuits. 'Help yourselves,' he told them, then settled himself in another chair. He had also been carrying a box file under his arm, which he put down and opened up.

'First of all – about Mangrove Flats,' he began. 'There is such a place, except no one calls it that any more. There's nothing there except mangroves, although twenty years ago it was a popular spot for hikers and campers. There were a few old fishermen's huts and holiday cottages but the mangroves grew everywhere, and the little bay where the sea came in is muddy and quite hard to get to.'

He opened up the file. Jenny and Simon watched quietly as he took out a photograph.

'The case has never been closed,' he said. 'It's an open file and at the time it was one of the most difficult cases I had ever encountered. Extra police were brought in to search the whole area. It was thought that maybe your mother had been injured, that maybe there had been an accident with the car, but there was nothing to go on. No sign of a car. You seemed to have just appeared from nowhere.' He put the photograph down on the table. 'Here, Jenny, this was you when we found you.'

Jenny picked it up and Simon leaned closer to look. The picture was of a small red-haired girl maybe two or three years old, wearing blue trousers and a blue jumper which had a koala on the front and was torn and dirty. Her hair was long and matted, she was filthy and wearing only one sneaker. She looked absolutely terrified.

Jenny tried to hold back the tears, and Sam put a box of tissues in front of her.

'Where was I?' she asked as she wiped her eyes.

'A couple of hikers found you sitting on the side of the road about a kilometre from Mangrove Flats. It seems they tried to find out where you'd come from and your name, but all you could say was "Mummy's gone" and that your name was Jenny. They searched around and found some campers but no one knew anything, so they did the right thing and brought you here.'

Sam pulled out some papers from the file. 'Here's their statement, but that's the gist of it. They certainly weren't suspect in any way and we sent them on their way. I went out and cruised around and spread the word among the locals and everybody joined in the search. We did find your missing shoe, though, back in the bush near some rocks so we had an idea which way you had come, but there were no other signs that you'd ever been there at all. More police were called in and every building and all around the area was searched thoroughly, but they found nothing.'

He sat back and regarded Jenny as she said, 'Didn't I know my full name and address?'

Sam looked through the file some more. 'All you could tell us was that your name was Jenny Baker, and you lived in Adelaide but that you didn't live there any more and you were going on a picnic with your mummy We tried to find out your mother's first name and you said it was Mummy. You said your car was blue and that it had stopped working.' He sighed, 'You have to realise that you were traumatised and hysterical. It took a long time to get those few facts. Oh,' he delved into the file again, 'you kept talking about a snake and Mummy telling you to run and hide. What is it, Jenny? Do you remember something?' Sam looked anxious as she jumped up and then sat down again,

'My dream,' she said. 'In my dream I was being chased by someone and I saw a hand coming towards me and there was a snake.' She stopped. 'But I can't remember anything else. It's all a blank.'

Sam put a big hand over hers. 'It must have been terrible. I'm not surprised you've blanked it all out. I was sad to see you go,' he continued now, 'so was my wife Pat. You stayed with us for a month while they investigated but there were no reports of any missing persons that fitted your description. Nothing.' He picked up Simon's photograph. 'If we can find this cottage, maybe it will trigger a memory.' He searched Jenny's face, 'Are you up to this, lass?'

She had dried her eyes and a look of determination had come over her face. 'Definitely,' she said. 'I want to know. I'll try to remember. Maybe something will come back.'

'Good girl,' Sam beamed. 'I'll tell you what, how about you two go and find some lunch somewhere – the pub does a good one. My constable will be back soon and then I'll take you along to Mangrove Flats in the four-wheel drive. It's pretty rough country out there and you don't want to mess up your nice clean little hatchback, do you?' He grinned. He had noticed Simon's white Toyota parked outside.

Simon smiled. 'Sounds good to me.' He turned to Jenny, eyebrows raised, and she nodded. 'How about we come back in an hour – say one o'clock, would that be okay?'

'Good thinking. Sounds like a plan. I'll see you later.' Sam saw them out of the door.

Jenny left it to Simon to find somewhere for lunch, but she could not eat much, her stomach was churning. Who knew what they might uncover. Would she remember anything? Part of her didn't want to know. But after they were seated in the pub and she had settled down a bit and had time to think, she had made up her mind

'I need to know,' she told Simon, 'no matter what.'

'Even it's something bad?'

'Yes, even if it's something bad.'

Four

After they had gone, Sam looked more carefully through the files. He drew out a newspaper cutting. LITTLE GIRL LOST was the headline, and the article asked if anyone recognised the child to get in touch with the police. There had been phone calls from many people who thought they might have recognised her. Each one was carefully checked out and all proved fruitless.

Sam had figured at the time that there was no way a mother would have abandoned her child voluntarily, especially one like Jenny who was well cared for and who obviously loved her mum, which left only one conclusion. Her mother had been taken by force and met with foul play. If she were still alive, she would have been looking for her child. He wondered how much Jenny had been told, whether she had ever contacted the police in later years. At the time, Jenny had been unable to tell them where the house was and where she had been.

One thing that had always bothered Sam was the fact that she had kept talking about a snake, but it had been wintertime and there were no snakes around. He had a plan now, though. It was just a hunch, but if he was right, it would be a breakthrough.

Going back to another file, Sam sorted through until he had found a photograph, then he put it inside an envelope and tucked it into his pocket. Maybe, he thought, this would be all that was needed to jog Jenny's memory.

Sam was waiting for them when they returned to the police station after lunch, and Jenny was feeling apprehensive as they climbed into the big four-wheel drive. It was only about ten minutes before they turned off onto an unsurfaced road, full of potholes and scrubby growth.

'This is the way to the old Mangrove Flats,' Sam told them. 'As you can see, the road's never been properly surfaced. Nnobody comes here any more.'

Jenny and Simon were looking out of the windows.

'It's a spooky looking place,' Simon remarked. He turned to Jenny, 'I don't suppose you remember anything much, do you? It was all so long ago.' He was holding the photograph of the old cottage and peering out of the window, trying to see through the trees and bushes.

'Stop!' Jenny had been peering out of the other side, and Sam braked.

'Do you recognise something?' he asked.

'I don't know.' She opened the door and stepped out, going to the side of the road for a better look, then returned quickly and climbed back in. 'No, sorry. I thought for a moment it was, but that was just an old corrugated-iron place and the one we're looking for is definitely a stone cottage, but it's hard to see anything through all the trees and bushes.' She was sounding defeated. 'I don't think this is going to work.'

They drove on slowly. There were a few more old shacks scattered around in disrepair and abandoned, then they passed another stone cottage but while it was in better condition than the other buildings; it was nothing like Simon's picture.

Sam had been silent for a bit. 'Hold on,' he said now and suddenly turned off the road onto another even more dilapidated track, leading between the trees, the branches brushing the sides of the vehicle. He stopped and pointed. 'What about this one then?'

They stared at an old cottage partly hidden behind the overgrown vegetation. There was no sign of a windmill; indeed, if there ever was one, it was long gone. The mangroves were blocking the end of the road and they couldn't drive any further.

Sam turned the engine off and all three of them climbed out of the vehicle and stood silently looking at the old building. It was quiet except for faint sucking sounds coming from the direction of the murky water creeping around the mangrove roots, and odd splashing noises.

Jenny shivered. 'This is it,' she said quietly. 'This is the house.'

It was a place of foreboding where you felt you had to speak in whispers in case you disturbed something. The air felt oppressive and there was a smell of rotting vegetation.

Simon broke the silence. He looked at the picture. 'Yes, this is definitely it.' He put his arm around Jenny, 'You okay, Jen?'

She nodded and Sam indicated the house.

'Well, if you're sure, we'd better see if we can get in and have a proper look. What d'you reckon, you two? Are you game?' Without waiting for an answer, he started clearing tree branches and brush, making his way along a path which was still partly visible.

As they followed him, Jenny tried hard to remember anything at all that seemed familiar as they approached the building.

Sam stopped as they reached a small clearing. 'What a mess!' he said. 'The vandals have been having a great time with this one.'

The windows were all smashed, the front door had disappeared and there was only half a roof left, but the chimney was still intact.

'I reckon this must have been a nice little cottage once,' remarked

Simon, He turned to Sam. 'Do you remember coming here when they did the searching?'

'As a matter of fact, I do. There was an old Holden ute outside which turned out to have been stolen. It wasn't in working order, though. The engine had had it.' He looked around and pointed, 'I can't believe it's still here. Looks like it's been stripped of anything worth taking.'

He led the way though the front door space into what would have been the main living area. They looked around. It had been thoroughly trashed. Broken furniture, graffiti, empty food containers and bottles were strewn around.

'It's disgusting how people can do this!' Jenny stood upright one of the chairs which wasn't broken.

'Squatters,' said Sam. 'Over the years they came and they went, but over time they stopped coming. I doubt the original owners are still alive. Iit's just an abandoned old house. There's no people coming to fish any more and I don't think there are any crabs, plus you can't swim unless you go out for a long way through the mangroves.' He turned to Jenny. 'Does anything at all ring a bell?' he asked her.

She shook her head, then went over and touched the bricks surrounding the big open fireplace. 'I don't know,' she said. 'I was so little and everything seemed to be so big. I'm not even sure this was the house, although I think I sort of maybe remember this fireplace.' She sighed. 'I'm not much help, I'm afraid.'

Sam was taking a photograph out of an envelope. He gave it to her. 'What about this?' he asked. 'Does this mean anything to you?'

He watched her closely as she studied the picture, then she stiffened, her face whitened, and she shakily handed it to Simon. She couldn't answer for a moment.

Then she whispered, 'it's the snake. It's the snake in my dream!'

'Here,' Sam brought the kitchen chair forward.

She sat down and looked at Simon, who was carefully examining the picture.

'Who is this?' he asked.

It was a photo of a man's arm with a snake tattooed around it down to his wrist, the snake's head ending up on the back of his hand. It was well done and very lifelike. It was no wonder, thought Simon, that it would look real to a child.

'Snake Wilson,' Sam replied. 'Nasty piece of work, been in and out of jail for years, break and enter, assault, you name it, he's done it. We had no reason to connect him with Jenny and her mum, though. At the time, he was thought to be in Perth, but Jenny,' he continued, 'after you mentioned a snake, it triggered my memory. It's a long shot, but now I think maybe he was holed up here, hiding from whoever was after him. It would have been something to do with drugs, if he was, that's for sure.'

'He tried to grab me,' Jenny blurted out, 'and Mummy said run and hide, so I ran and he tried to catch me. That's when I must have seen the snake.' A look of terror passed over her face, then she closed her eyes and took a few deep breaths.

Simon brought her a bottle of water from his backpack.

'Thanks.' Jenny took a drink.

'Well done, Jenny,' Sam smiled. 'Is there anything else coming back? Why do you think your mum told you to run?'

'I don't know.' She looked distressed. 'The rest is a blur. I'm sorry. I don't even remember where I went after that, or how I got to be on the road.'

Then she asked the question that had been with her since she was ten years old and her parents had told her she had been adopted. 'So what do think happened to my mum then?'

She looked at Sam, who was unable to answer. He looked at Simon and then they both looked at Jenny, who in a surprisingly calm voice said, 'It's all right. I'm not stupid, you know. If my mother had been alive, she would have found me, I know that. I've always known it. I just haven't really thought about it for a long time, not since the nightmares stopped when I was a child. I think I just accepted something I could do nothing about. But now I need to know the truth. I want to know what happened to her.'

She watched Sam, who was looking somewhat relieved to know that he didn't have to give her false hope, and that perhaps, after all this time, maybe he could find some way of closing this case. Now that Snake Wilson was in the picture, there was something else to go on, to follow up.

Simon gazed at her admiringly. 'You're amazing, Jen.' He went over to the filthy sink, trying the tap because his water bottle was empty, not that he really expected to find drinkable water but he was curious. 'Where did they get their water from, inspector? There's no water main, is there?'

'They would have been connected to a water tank, I guess, and there may have been a well. 'Sam looked thoughtful. 'Why?'

'Nothing, just an idea.' Simon looked at Jenny, who had a determined look on her face as she got to her feet.

'The snake wasn't real then, was it? It must have seemed real to me at the time. Inspector,' she continued, 'is there anything else they found in the original investigation that I should be told about? My parents told me how I was found but it was never really mentioned after that and I guess I never asked questions.'

'OK, Jenny.' He took a breath. 'First of all, I think it's time you both called me Sam like everybody else around here. Now,' he continued, 'I have to tell you that after all the searches and the lack of any other information we had to assume that...' He trailed off and Jenny finished the sentence. '

So you had to assume that she was dead.' There, she'd said it, her worst thoughts, but now there were no tears, just a sense of determination in her voice as she studied the policeman. 'And I would like you to keep me fully up to date with anything else you find out. Would that be OK, insp...um...Sam?' she asked him.

'For sure, no worries.'

Simon had been listening with interest. Suddenly, he headed for the door.

'Where are you going, Simon?' Jenny started to follow him.

'Just for a look around. A hunch, stupid probably. It's certain to already have been searched. But Sam, that ute – what d'you reckon is underneath it? Do you know if it was moved?'

Sam shook his head. 'Don't know. I don't think so.' He regarded Simon, eyebrows raised in question. 'You're thinking about a well?'

They were all having the same thoughts now as they approached the old ute. Tall weeds and years of growth surrounded the vehicle and it was going to take more manpower than they could manage. Both men got down and tried to clear it a little but…

'We'll need some help shifting this.' Sam stood up. 'It's worth a look, but not today. You guys have to get back to Adelaide. I'll get a couple of blokes and organise something tomorrow, then I promise I'll be in touch, no matter if we find something or not. OK?' He looked at Jenny, who nodded.

Then she had a thought. 'I'd like to have a look around the back. I've just remembered something else. I must have been hiding somewhere.'

They followed her to the back of the house, and she stopped and pointed.

'It's still there.' She couldn't go any closer. 'The old dunny. I think that's where I hid. There were spiderwebs.' She covered her face, and then it all came out in a rush, 'I waited for Mum to come for such a long time, but she didn't come and then I heard the car start and I ran out but it went up the road and left me behind.'

'Oh, my God.' Simon put his arm around her. 'Then you must have thought she had gone and forgotten all about you.'

Sam was shaking his head. No wonder the poor little kid had been hysterical.

They were both quiet on the drive back to Berriwell. They said their goodbyes.

'Thanks, Sam, for everything,' Jenny said as they shook hands.

'See you soon. Take care on the road back,' Sam told them as they left.

Five

It was with a sense of foreboding mixed with hope that Sam and two stocky blokes from the wrecking yard arrived at Mangrove Flats the following day. They set to work, clearing rubbish and vegetation from around the old ute. Then they attached a rope to their truck and heaved away until it was clear.

Sam saw what he had been hoping for. Under the debris was a wooden lid flush with the ground and covering a hole just over a metre in diameter. It was firmly embedded, and they had to prise it off before slipping it sideways, revealing a black hole. The stench coming out was foul and Sam covered his nose as he bent over to have a look.

It didn't seem to be all that deep. He threw down a rock, which landed with a dry thud.

'No water,' he remarked. 'Someone's going to have to go down.' He looked at one of the men. 'Robbo, are you up for this?'

'Piece of cake,' that worthy replied. 'Used to go abseiling back in the day. I'll fetch some rope.'

Sam grinned. 'Off you go then.'

They tied the rope around a nearby tree, and Robbo lowered himself down.

It didn't take long before a hail came from below.

'Bring me up.'

When they got him back to the top again, Robbo had a handbag slung over his shoulder. 'It's not good, Sam,' he said. 'There's a body down there. Woman, looks like, judging from the clothes. This bag was on the top, and there's a suitcase there as well. She's pretty well wedged in.' He looked upset as he added, 'We'll have to get the ambos in, looks like, and some lifting equipment. How long d'you think she's been there?'

'About twenty-five years.' Sam patted Robbo on the back. 'It's a long story, mate. I'll take it from here, and thanks again for a good job. You two can be off now.'

After they had gone, Sam fixed his crime scene tape around the well, put the handbag into a big plastic one and carefully stowed it into his car. He was going to have to make that phone call, but work had to be done first. It would be difficult and nasty and create a lot of paperwork. He sighed.

Snake Wilson was not too difficult to locate. He was back in jail again, as Sam discovered after just one phone call, so he decided to go and interview him personally, making arrangements to fly interstate in a couple of days.

Meanwhile, the body of a woman was finally extricated from the well, along with her belongings, which were stashed in the Berriwell police station. Her clothes, along with her daughter's, were in the suitcase, and the contents of her handbag had birth and death certificates, along with other documents which Sam thought Jenny needed to see.

He made the phone call Wednesday evening.

'Hello, Sam.' Jenny said, and then waited for him to speak.

'I'm sorry, Jenny,' he started, 'but it seems Simon's hunch was right. There was a well, and we found your mum's body.' There was no other way than to say it straight out and he waited for her to speak.

'Oh,' she sounded shaky and was quiet for a few seconds. 'Are you sure?' she asked then.

'As sure as we can be, but forensics and DNA have come a long way in the past twenty-five years and there are documents which establish her identification as Christine Baker.' He waited. He could hear someone speaking in the background and hoped it was Judy, the friend Jenny had told him about. She would need some support just now.

But her voice was steady now as she asked next, 'So where is she now then?'

'Here in the morgue. I have her suitcase, which was also in the well, along with her handbag containing documents which I think will be important for you to see. Can you come to Berriwell and collect everything?'

'Yes, of course.' Jenny asked her next question. 'What about that Snake Wilson person?'

'He's in jail and I'm going to interview him tomorrow, Thursday. Maybe when I see you next I'll have some answers. Jenny?'

'Yes.'

'Are you okay?'

'Yes, I'm fine,' she told him. 'Would next Sunday be all right? Otherwise I'll have to get time off from work.'

'That sounds like a plan. I'll see you – and Simon? – when you get here.'

'Thanks, Sam, and thanks for everything. And yes, probably Simon as well.'

The tears came for a little while after she had hung up the phone.

'At least you know now.' Judy, ever practical, was making tea. 'Here.' she said, 'have a cuppa, and a tissue.' Then she sat down alongside her friend until she had told her everything and dried her eyes.

'I'm going over next Sunday,' Jenny sipped her tea, 'to collect her things.'

'Would you like me to come with you?'

'Thanks, Jude, but Simon has offered to drive me if I have to go back.' She picked up the phone. 'I'd better let him know what's happened.'

Judy smiled. She had met Simon and thoroughly approved.

They were on their way back to Berriwell the following Sunday. Jenny had been unable to settle over the past few days and needed to know all the details now. The fact that her mother had not voluntarily left her was a small consolation and only confirmed what she always knew in her heart.

'I hope Sam managed to find out what happened.' She repeated out loud what she had been thinking.'

'He's a good copper, is Sam,' Simon told her. 'He'll have found out everything, you'll see.'

They arrived late morning, and the inspector was waiting. His face broke into a smile as Jenny gave him a hug. It seemed to be the right thing to do. He felt like an old friend.

'Come on in.' He looked anxiously at Jenny. 'How are you coping?'

'I'm fine, Sam, thanks,' she reassured him.

He led them into the back room of the police station, where there was an old brown battered suitcase and a black handbag on the table.

Jenny eyed them uncertainly. 'Is this them? Can I open them now, or should I take them home and do it later?'

'Up to you. The suitcase is full of clothes, but I think you'll want to have a look in the bag, when you're alone. There are documents which may help solve some of your questions about your past. But you want to hear about Snake Wilson, don't you? So here's the plan,' Sam continued. 'Pat, my wife, is wanting to catch up with you and is hoping you'll both come for lunch. Also, my son Greg is home on leave from the army, and remembers well the little red-headed sister he had for a short time.' Sam looked expectantly at Jenny. 'So what do you say?'

She looked at Simon, who asked her what she would like to do. 'I'd love to catch up with Pat,' she said, 'so thanks, Sam, yes, that would be lovely, and,' she added, 'I'll take the bags home to look at later, if that's OK?'

Sam nodded. 'So that's settled.' He looked happy. 'I'll let her know we'll be home in an hour.'

He made a quick phone call, then, 'Now about Snake Wilson,' he said. 'Yes, I found him. He's in the prison hospital. He's a mess. Drugs, booze, everything's caught up with him. He's got lung cancer and he knows he hasn't got long. It took a little persuading, mind, but in the end I got a confession and a statement from him which he signed. At first he wouldn't admit to anything but I showed him your picture, Jenny, and I think that's what made him come clean.' Sam stopped talking for a moment as he gathered his thoughts.

'It was strange. It was as if maybe he wanted to get it off his chest and once he started talking he kept going.' Sam opened a file which he had in front of him. 'Perhaps it would be best if I read his statement.'

Jenny and Simon both nodded at the same time.

So he continued. 'Time and date were confirmed. By the way, his real name is Humphrey James Wilson,' Sam told them, then went on, 'This is what he said he remembered: "Well, the ute which I'd borrowed – well, OK, nicked – was cactus, it wouldn't restart, so I was stuck at the house without transport. I had a big pile of stuff which I had to bag up to take to WA, where I had a customer waiting. When the woman came to the door with the kid, she wanted directions, said she was lost and was looking for the picnic grounds. Well, I didn't know nuffin' about no picnic grounds and I told her so and I was trying to get to get rid of them when I saw her looking through the door at the stuff on the table behind me. I could tell she knew what it was and she started to turn round to go away, but I couldn't risk it. She could've gone straight to the cops, so I grabbed her and told her to get inside, plus I'd seen her car and had an idea.

'"The kid was hanging on to the mother and I dragged them both inside. If the woman had kept her cool, it would have been OK, but no, she started making a fuss when I told her I wanted to borrow her car. She started getting mad, then she said she wouldn't tell the cops anything and that she would give me a ride, but you can't trust a woman to keep her mouth shut, can you, so I decided to tie them up while I got away.

'"Then she told the kid to make a run for it and I tried to grab her but she was too quick and got out through the door ,which hadn't shut properly. Then when the woman tried to follow the kid, she slipped and fell and her head hit the rocks around the fireplace. There was blood and she had stopped breathing, so I knew then she was done for. I looked outside for the kid but she had gone. So I finished bagging the stuff and got the car keys from the woman's bag and took the cash from her purse.

'"I was going to leave her there and scarper, but changed my mind. It was better to get rid of all the evidence, in case the kid came back with someone else, so I got rid of the rocks which had blood on them, and then she went down the well and the bags on top. I put the lid back on, then managed to push the ute over it. The kid had disappeared but there were people coming and going around there so

I knew she'd be found but I couldn't take the risk of her leading them back to the house.

'"Then I took the car and got out of there, but was halfway across the Nullarbor when it got a puncture, didn't it, and there was no spare, so I had to get it onto the side of the road. Then I put a light to it, torched it. I got another ride from a truckie who didn't give a stuff and asked no questions, which suited me fine."'

Sam stopped for a moment and said, 'I told him then that you had survived, and that you had spent your life wondering what had happened to your mother, and then he said, "I done a lot of bad stuff in me life, but I never killed a woman and I never hurt a kid."

'Then he signed the statement, and I thanked him. Then he said, "Tell the kid I'm sorry."' Sam stopped talking.

Jenny and Simon were quiet.

Then Jenny said, 'So she wasn't murdered, she fell, but he was still going to leave us there, stranded. What a monster!' She could say no more. It was all too much to think about right now.

'So they never found the car?' Simon asked. Then realised, 'I guess there'd be a lot of cars abandoned over there on the Nullarbor, wouldn't there, and I suppose if it was torched it would be hard to find the owner,'

Sam nodded., 'That's true, Simon. If someone wanted to cover their tracks back then, that's one way go about it. Happens a lot, even today.' Sam rose and picked up the handbag from the table. 'We'd better get cracking and get on home for lunch. You could lock this in your car along with the suitcase, then you can go straight back home afterwards. We've got all we need for identification purposes from the information in here,' he indicated the bag, 'and taken copies for the records. We also have a nice big thumbprint which I am one hundred per cent sure will be Snake Wilson's. In any case. his signed statement is good enough to close this case as far as your mother's disappearance is concerned.'

Jenny was quiet on the short drive over to Sam's house, but as soon as she saw Pat, who gave her a warm embrace, and Greg, who scooped her up in a big hug, then entered the enormous kitchen with the big family-size table, memories came back.

It was a great reunion. She had to admit she couldn't really remember what any of the family had looked like. She had tried to remember Sam as he used to be, but he had lost nearly all of his hair, and Pat, who used to be thin, most definitely wasn't now. Greg, of course, was all grown-up. People change in twenty-five years, but she remembered the kitchen, the cooking smells and the feeling of home. She sat down on a kitchen chair and looked around. How could she have forgotten? But she knew. It was all connected with a nightmare time that she had tried so hard to forget.

Lunch was a happy affair. They didn't talk about the past. Sam rightly guessed it was all too raw for Jenny at the moment, so he told them about his soon-to-be retirement, and Greg's future in the army and Pat's voluntary work in the community, just general things, until it was time to leave, with invitations to come back soon.

As he saw them to the car, Sam stopped and spoke quietly. 'As soon as the autopsy is done and the body is ready to he released, I'll let you know, and then perhaps you'll want to make arrangements for the funeral. We'd be happy to have it here in Berriwell, if you like, in the local church. Just think about it, OK? Whatever you decide, we would all like to be there.' He gave her a hug and then shook Simon's hand. 'You'll look after this little lady, won't you, Simon?' he said.

Simon smiled. 'No worries on that score. I intend to do just that.'

Jenny cradled the handbag in her lap all the way home. She was tempted to open it but waited; the time wasn't right.

They didn't talk much on the way back, and when they finally arrived, Simon fetched the suitcase out of the boot, saw her to the door and gave her a kiss on the cheek.

'Call me, OK?'

'I will. Maybe tomorrow.'

'Take care,' he said.

Judy wasn't home but had left a note on the table letting her know that she would be home around 8 p.m. and hoping that Jenny's day had gone well. So she made herself a coffee, opened the suitcase, and did a quick sort through the clothes. They were all mildewed, damp and smelly, so she closed the case, then looked at the handbag.

It had been what looked like black leather that had gone green with mildew, and a brass clasp which was rusty. It wasn't quite closed and she wondered how the police had managed to open it. The contents were old, faded and damp. Jenny looked in the wallet, which was mouldy, and at the cards inside. The plastic had stood the test of time and she found credit and savings cards. There was a driver's licence in the name of Christine Baker.

'Christine,' she murmured.

There were other cards which she didn't recognise and she put them aside. There was a small make-up bag green with mould and full of cosmetics, fit for nothing but the bin. There were other sundries but nothing of note.

Jenny had been leaving an envelope for last and she opened it carefully. Birth certificate, death certificate and a couple of letters. Carefully she looked first at the birth certificates, the writing faint but readable. Her birthday was 10 July 1989. That meant, she calculated, that she was nearly three years old when she was found. Mother, Christine Anne Baker, she read, and father, Thomas George Baker, of Pingeraboo, Northern Territory.

Carefully she opened the next document. It was a death certificate for Thomas George Baker, cause of death injuries received when thrown from a horse at Pingeraboo in 1991. Jennny tried to remember her father, but there was nothing. How could she forget her father? Tears came then. How come she had never known any of this?

Next there was a marriage licence. Her parents had been married in Dundee, Scotland, in 1986. Jenny felt a twinge of excitement. Had she got grandparents in Scotland then?

She tried to figure it out. So they had come to Australia, they lived somewhere called Pingeraboo, she had been born and her father had died. Then her mother must have driven to Adelaide.

There was a letter inside a separate envelope, addressed TO WHOM IT MAY CONCERN. Written in beautiful copperplate writing, it appeared to be a reference for employment, saying that Christine Baker was an excellent cook/housekeeper, was reliable and honest, and highly recommended for any position of this nature. The last letter was from an employment agency in Perth, confirming the date of an interview on 7 June. Jenny put the letter down with the others and sighed. So she was going for a job, looks like, she thought.

Suddenly she got up and opened the suitcase again. 'There's got to be photos,' she muttered, and rummaged around in the bottom. 'Aha!' she exclaimed, and there it was, an old photo album, mouldy of course, but she opened it up. There were wedding pictures, family pictures, all sorts dating from who knew when, but some were still clear enough to see, a lot in black and white and very faded sepia. She was still going through it when Judy came home, and she brought her friend up to date with everything that had happened that day.

The funeral was held at the Uniting church at Berriwell. Sam organised everything and his family were there, including Greg and his sister Susan, who had travelled from Perth. Simon drove Jenny and Judy over, and a few folk from Berriwell who, remembering the time when a little girl was found near Mangrove Flats, turned up as well. Jenny's adoptive parents arrived the day before, anxious to see Jenny and really happy to see the mystery of their beloved daughter's past finally resolved.

After the simple service, they all went back to Sam's place for a sort of wake and remembrance, and they raised glasses to the memory of Christine.

Later on, Sam announced his retirement date, which was to be very soon. He was happy that his baffling cold case had finally been resolved. The fatal damage to Christine's skull corresponded with the account given by Snake Wilson, who had apparently passed away shortly after making his confession. Jenny was relieved that her mother had died immediately without any suffering.

After things had got back to normal, she thought, she might take a trip over to Scotland to try to track down any other relatives she may have. In the meanwhile, he would be going back to her painting class.

Simon, though, was thinking of other things besides painting classes, which involved Jenny making a decision. But he was a patient guy; he didn't mind waiting.

So perhaps it was all the beginning of a happy ending.

Blind Date

'When did you last go on a date?' Tommo asked Ben.

They were having a beer at the local pub.

'Can't remember. Why?' Ben asked him.

'Well, how would you feel about going on a blind date with me and Shirl?'

'Well, I dunno. A blind date? You mean I don't get to see her until we get there? Where are you going? What's she like? That's a bit of a risk, mate. Anyway, I've done with women since the missus shot through. I've kind of lost interest.'

'Well, first of all,' Tommo started, 'it's my birthday. Second, we're going to the Grand Hotel. And third, Shirl reckons that this is a real nice girl. Short and sweet, pretty and intelligent.'

'If she's so amazing, how come she hasn't got a boyfriend?' Ben was scathing. 'What's the catch? I mean, why would you ask me? Anyway, what does she do?'

'She works with Shirl on the telephone helpline. And she's new, she doesn't know anyone here. She's come down from Queensland,' Tommo explained. 'Plus you're my best mate.'

'Well, have you met her?' Ben was still dubious.

'No, I haven't, but I trust Shirl's judgement.'

"Well, OK then, I guess.' Ben gave in. 'Saturday night, did you say? What time?'

'Say 6.30. and wear something decent, Ben. Have you got a good shirt?'

'Course I have. What d'you take me for? A moron?'

So Ben made a big effort. He didn't go out for a proper dinner very often. Well, come to think of it, he really couldn't remember the last time. Maccas and Pizza Hut and pies at the pub were not really restaurants, he supposed.

Anyway, he found his good blue striped shirt, sniffed it and held it up to make sure there weren't any stains he hadn't noticed, showered and shaved and even ironed his good daks. He wondered about a tie. He had a couple of ties. One had chickens on it and the other was his local footy team colours. He rolled up the footy one and put it in his jacket pocket, just in case. He had a good jacket, as it happened, almost the same colour as his pants. He couldn't remember the last time he had worn a jacket. He looked at himself in the bedroom mirror and decided that he would have to do.

Ben was feeling nervous. He was awkward around women. He could never think of things to say. He was conscious of his balding pate and his widening girth. He pulled his stomach in and realised he could only just about do up the buttons. He sighed. 'Let's just get this over with,' he muttered.

Ben arrived at the hotel in good time and ventured into the restaurant, hoping that he wouldn't be the first to arrive. Then he saw Tommo, who was in the bar area, waving at him.

He looked Ben over. 'Well, you scrubbed up OK,' he said approvingly.

Ben grinned. 'Happy birthday, mate. Well, I had to make a bit of an effort, didn't I? This place is a bit fancy!' He looked around. 'Well, where are they then?'

'In the Ladies.' Tommo had a funny look on his face as he started to say, 'Um…maybe there's something…' but he didn't finish. His wife Shirley and another person were walking towards them.

Ben stared at the girl, who was absolutely gorgeous. Petite, long dark hair and wearing a blue outfit that clung to, in Ben's opinion, an amazing figure.

'Hi, Ben.' Shirley smiled at him. She was very fond of Ben. She had known him almost as long as she had known Tommo, and she worried about him.

'Hi, Shirl.' He gave her a kiss on the cheek and then turned towards the girl.

'Ben,' said Shirl, 'I'd like you to meet Annie. Annie, this is Ben.'

He held out his hand but she took no notice. In fact, she seemed to be looking over his shoulder at someone else. He half turned to look behind him but Tommo touched his arm and indicated the white stick Annie was holding.'

Ben stared for a moment and, as realisation dawned, he saw Annie's hand reaching towards him.

'Hello, Ben,' she said in a strong Irish accent. 'Nice to meet you.'

He grasped her hand, but couldn't speak for a moment then, gathering himself together, he replied, 'Nice to meet you too, Annie. What part of Ireland are you from, then?'

They were soon chatting about Ireland where, fortunately, Ben had family. He managed to cast an accusing look at Tommo with a promise of 'I'll get you for this later' in his eyes. Then they were told their table was ready and called for dinner.

Tommo looked over at Shirl and winked, and she smiled back. They were watching Ben, who suddenly was full of confidence. He was taking charge, holding Annie's arm and guiding her along. He was talking animatedly and she was happily responding.

'Didn't you tell him she was blind?' Shirl whispered.

'Well, I told him it was a blind date, didn't I?' said Tommo with a smirk. 'And by the way, that was a brilliant idea you had, Shirl. It seems to be working.'

Miracle Grass

Humphrey Snodgrass was very particular about his lawn. He tended it with care and had a big KEEP OFF THE GRASS sign on a stick stuck right in the middle, just in case a visitor decided to take a short cut across the lawn instead of walking up the driveway.

The local kids sometimes chucked rubbish over the front fence just to see him jump up and shout at them. 'Off with you,' he'd yell, and they'd run away laughing as he carefully made his way across the grass to pick up the discarded cans or whatever, muttering threats meant to deter them, though they never did.

Indeed, he was a strange and fearsome sight when he was angry, in spite of his small stature. His beard was long and straggly, with patches of grey beginning to show. His hair hung over his ears and a bald patch was creeping slowly over the top towards the back, although it was usually hidden behind a battered old sun hat. In fact, he rather resembled one of the strange-looking gnomes which he had placed carefully around the edges of the lawn, guarding the succulents.

Next door to Humphrey lived Joe Parsons. Joe's lawn was bare most of the time. Mainly because he didn't water it. Joe wasn't a gardening person and he felt a bit guilty every time he looked over the fence and saw Humphrey's immaculate lawn, He also had not missed his neighbour's disdainful glance which he had cast over Joe's lawn whenever they had a chat over the fence. This by the way, was difficult for Humphrey, as he had to stand on an upturned crate, but Joe, being a tall strapping young man, had no problem with having a look now and again. Joe bore no grudges, though. He had more to worry about, he thought, than the state of his lawn.

One day, Joe made a plan. Humphrey had told him that he was

going away for a week to visit his sister in Queensland. He had checked the weather and rain was forecast, so he decided that the lawn would survive quite well for a few days without watering. He asked Joe if he would keep an eye on the place. 'You don't need to water,' he said, 'just look out for rubbish.'

'No worries,' said Joe. 'I'll keep an eye on things. You just go off and have a good time.'

So on Friday, Humphrey caught a cab to the airport, casting an anxious eye on the lawn before leaving.

The next day, some guys came in a truck and, after doing a bit of work levelling out Joe's lawn and getting rid of rubbish and rocks, they rolled out some grass, and settled it into place. It looked quite beautiful, lush and green.

Joe looked over the fence at Humphrey's lawn. 'Looks as good as his now,' he said to his girlfriend, who was visiting, 'Old Snooty can't turn his nose up at my lawn any more.'

The next weekend when Humphrey returned, he first thing he did of course was to check the lawn. A few weeds had sprung up, and he frowned as he noticed a few bare patches here and there but otherwise everything seemed to be OK.

So it wasn't until the next day – when he had a look over the fence to see if Joe was there, which he wasn't, to thank him for keeping an eye on things – that he noticed the lawn. Humphrey nearly fell off the crate as he gave a great gasp of surprise. Joe's lawn had been transformed; it was lush and green. In fact, the grass looked even thicker than his own. He couldn't believe it. How could grass grow so quickly in a week? Humphrey felt completely unravelled and, shaking with disbelief, he had to go inside and sit down for a bit.

That evening he listened for Joe's car, and hurried outside to climb onto his crate. 'Excuse me,' he called, just as Joe got out of his car. 'Just wanted to thank you for keeping an eye on everything.'

'Hi, Mr Snodgrass.' Joe smiled. 'It's been all quiet here, no problems. Did you have a good week, then?'

'Yes, thank you. Um…' Humphrey hesitated. 'I see you have a new lawn,' he said, trying not to sound as if it was too important.

'Oh, yes,' Joe waved at the lawn. 'Looks good, doesn't it? It's a special new seed you can get now. Just sprinkle it on and it comes up in a few days. You have to do it when it's raining, though, or it takes a bit longer.'

'What's it called, then?' Humphrey asked now, desperate to know.

'It's called Miracle Grass.' Joe turned away with a smile, but couldn't resist adding, 'Looks nearly as good as yours now, doesn't it?'

Humphrey humphed as he turned away and hurried indoors. He wrote Miracle Grass in his notebook.

The next day, he headed for the gardening department in the local shopping centre. 'Do you stock Miracle Grass seed?' he asked.

'Miracle Grass seed? No, sir, I've never heard of it, but to make sure, I'll check with the manager.'

Humphrey waited, fidgeting anxiously until the salesman returned.

'No, sir, sorry we don't stock it,' he said. 'You could try the garden centre,' he added helpfully.

Humphrey, feeling not a little disgruntled, headed to the nearest garden centre. It was a big nursery with a huge variety of plants.

Humphrey posed his question, adding, 'It grows a full lawn in a week. I've seen it.'

The young man looked doubtful. 'Well, sir,' he said, 'I don't know of any seed that will grow grass that fast. Some will come up pretty quick with maybe plenty of watering, but not that quick. If you know of a seed that will do that, then I'd like to know about it. If it exists,' he added with a smirk.

Humphrey drove back home feeling angry and confused. Had he been made a fool of? He had another look over the front gate at Joe's lawn as he drove slowly past. It looked pretty normal, He compared it with his and had to admit that Joe's grass was now looking better than his own, which had more and more bare patches appearing in a few places.

He headed indoors in such a bad temper he could scarcely contain himself. Why would Joe mislead him like that? Why had he given him the wrong name. What was the big secret?

So Humphrey made a plan. He would get a sample of grass and take it to the nursery, who would then be able to tell him what kind of seed it came from. So the next morning, he listened for Joe's car departing. As soon as the coast was clear, Humphrey headed down the drive and went next door. He opened the gate and carefully walked onto the beautiful lush green grass. Frowning thoughtfully, he bent over and pulled. It was firmly rooted in the ground, but he tugged hard and a small cluster finally came loose.

Humphrey sniffed at it then put on his reading glasses, which he kept in his top pocket, and peered closely. It didn't smell like grass at all and it certainly didn't feel like it. Plus it didn't actually have any soil attached to the bottom.

He slowly realised the truth. Hurriedly he dropped the grass onto the ground and made his way back home feeling totally humiliated and disgusted. How could he have been so stupid? Truth be told, he had never encountered fake grass before, but he had indeed heard of it.

He never said anything to Joe; he wouldn't give him the satisfaction. He just kept tending his lawn, putting potting mix and more normal seed over his lawn and, with watering, the bare patches gradually disappeared. He been tempted on one occasion to paint a sign with FAKE GRASS on it and stick it onto Joe's lawn, but decided against it, content in the fact that at least his lawn was real and not pretend.

Summer was a hot one that year. Humphrey liked to sit on his veranda in the evening with a beer after the sun had passed over to the back of the house. He liked to watch the sprinklers dancing over his lawn, which was beginning to look beautiful again.

One afternoon, he heard Joe come home and disappear into the house. He had noticed that his neighbour had a habit lately of going inside, stripping off his work clothes and changing into his shorts and running barefooted over his lawn to the mailbox. Perched unnoticed on his crate, Humphrey saw a lot.

Today the temperature had reached forty degrees. It was still very hot. Suddenly there was a great yell of anguish from Joe's garden and, concerned but not surprised in view of his recently acquired knowledge relating to fake lawns, Humphrey went over to the fence, climbed on to his box, and looked over.

Joe was hopping up and down, yelling and appearing to be in great pain with burning feet from the hot synthetic grass.

Humphrey gave an evil chuckle as he went back to his chair and picked up his cold beer. 'Cheers!' he said.

The Chocolate Cake

Abigail Harrington-Smith generally didn't generally hold with markets. In her experience, fishermen's markets were all right, as you could be sure the fish was fresh, also farmer's markets where they sold fresh fruit and vegetables, but markets with stalls and people selling, in Abigail's opinion, a miscellaneous collection of rubbish, were a waste of time. You ended up with stuff you didn't really need just because it seemed like a good bargain. Which was why, when she saw the large gathering of people and the stalls on the town oval which she passed on her home from the library, she was not intending to stop.

Cars were lined up along both sides of the road, however, so Abigail had to stop and wait to give a car room while it reversed out of a parking space. The car behind her was hooting loudly, no doubt thinking that, as she didn't have her blinkers on, she was going straight ahead and then he would be able to take the park. But Abigail had made a quick decision. As soon as the car vacated the spot, she put her blinkers on and moved straight into it. The irate car driver behind gave another hoot as he passed but she ignored him.

She sat for a moment chiding herself. She didn't know why she had stopped. Perhaps it was some perverse part of her brain that had wanted to thwart that mad hooting person from getting the park.

Well, I'm here now, she thought, so I may as well go in. Abigail took a plastic bag from the glovebox, folded it up and tucked it inside her handbag, just in case she needed it, then locked the car and made her way through the gate. She looked with distaste at the muddy ground. Recent rain had left a mess of puddles and she picked her way around them.

She stopped at the first stall and wrinkled her nose at the array of knick-knacks, assorted pieces of pottery, and kitchenware. Rubbish, she thought. Who needs this stuff? Abigail never bought anything second-hand. You never know where it's been, she'd say. She gave a cursory glance at another stall – pot plants; her gardener saw to all that sort of thing. She looked more closely at the handmade jewellery stall, and looked away again. Her two ex-husbands had provided her with more jewellery than she would ever need.

Suddenly she stopped. There was a cake stall. Abigail prided herself on her cake baking. At the afternoon teas she hosted occasionally for the town's progress committee, she always produced a home-made perfectly baked cake. Sometimes an impeccable sponge, or scones, light as a feather. It was her turn tomorrow and she would be baking a cake after she arrived home today.

The cakes on this stall, though, were, even by Abigail's standards, excellent. There had apparently been a competition for the best decorated cake and the winner's blue ribbon lay in front of an exquisite-looking chocolate cake with an intricate chocolate and white icing decoration on the top.

The young lady seated at the back of the stall smiled at her. 'All the cakes have been donated and they're for sale,' she said, 'and the proceeds go to local charities. Would you like to buy one?'

Abigail was torn. The $20 cost was a fair price. Maybe just this once she could break her rule. She decided she wouldn't bake tonight after all. 'All right, I'll take that one,' she said, indicating the chocolate cake.

It was on a paper plate covered with a clear plastic lid. Abigail handed over the money and, pulling out her folded shopping bag, settled the cake in the bottom.

Finding nothing else of any interest at the market, she made her way back to her car, then, after carefully placing the cake bag on the passenger seat, Abigail drove home.

She placed the cake on one of her best serving platters and put it in the fridge.

Next afternoon, Abigail's matching crockery stood on the embroidered tablecloth on the dining table, where the cake, looking quite splendid, waited for the ladies to arrive.

'My goodness, Abigail,' Anne, the committee's chairperson exclaimed, 'you really have surpassed yourself this time! That cake looks absolutely delicious.' She drew forward another visitor. 'This is Julia Barns,' she said. 'Julia's come to join us today. As we're one short on the committee, I'm hoping to persuade her to become a member.'

Abigail smiled and held out her hand. 'Welcome,' she said.

They shook hands and then Julia noticed the cake. 'The cake looks lovely,' she remarked.

'Thank you.' Abigail replied.

'Oh, Abigail bakes them herself, you know,' Anne enthused. 'She's an amazing cook. We always look forward to our meetings here. Her cakes are better than any of us can aspire to.'

Then other people were arriving and Abigail basked in their praise. 'It must have taken a long time to do that beautiful icing on top,' they said, 'and we can't wait to taste,' and so on, and so it went.

Indeed, the cake tasted as good as it looked. The meeting was very successful and Julia was persuaded to be nominated as a member at the upcoming AGM.

So Abigail was feeling very happy. Until the next day, that is. She had pulled the weekly local newspaper out of her letter box. As she skimmed through, she stopped at a page with an article about a recent charity fund-raising event at the local oval.

There were photographs of some of the stalls, how much money had been raised, and then a picture of the cake stall. There was the chocolate cake, in full colour in all its glory. 'Baked and donated by local resident Julia Barns', it said.

Horace Merryweather's Day

Relentless cold seeped through the walls of the modest fibro house and Horace Merryweather switched on the small electric heater. He set the oven timer, which would beep in half an hour, and then he would switch the heater off again. If he closed all the doors and made sure the windows were shut properly, there would be enough warmth in the room to last for a while.

It had been difficult getting out of bed this morning. The bedroom had become cold during the night but his bed was warm. He had been tempted to stay there and not get up at all. But that wouldn't do. Suppose someone came to the door, he thought; it would be so embarrassing if he was still in his pyjamas. Not that anyone ever came to his door, and the few family members he had left would always phone before dropping in. Anyway, he had always got up and dressed every morning; it was what one did.

So Horace carried out his usual morning routine then sat down for breakfast. It was Sunday today and he had an egg on toast, his usual Sunday breakfast. The rest of the week it was cereal. He turned on the radio. He left it on just long enough to listen to the news and hear the weather forecast. The news wasn't much different to yesterday and the weather forecast was for possible snow later in the day.

Horace sighed. He was feeling a bit down and depressed. When was this dreadful winter going to be over? He decided he had better get going to the shop before the weather changed for the worse. He always went down to the corner mini-market on Sundays to get the newspaper. He didn't bother much during the week, but on Sundays there were the supplements, which gave him something to read that wasn't about politics or murders, or famous people doing stuff which wasn't really anyone else's business. It filled up newspapers, he supposed, but didn't interest Horace in the slightest.

He passed a few people on the way, all looking miserable and huddled up in overcoats and scarves. No head nodding or polite greetings today; everyone was bent upon going about their business as quickly as possible.

Mrs Thompson greeted him with her usual cheerful self, though. She always seemed pleased to see him. She had run the shop on her own with the help of one assistant since Mr Thompson had passed away, and even did deliveries in her little blue van for people who couldn't get about.

'How are you, Mr Merryweather?' she asked, and Horace gave his usual reply, 'Fine, thank you, Mrs Thompson.'

He had been going to the same shop every Sunday, sometimes during the week and every pension day when he bought his groceries, for at least ten years. Yet the old -fashioned formalities persisted. For a fleeting moment, he wondered if it was time he asked Mrs Thompson to call him Horace.

Back home again, he made himself a cup of tea and turned the heater on again for another half hour, then opened his paper. He skimmed through the first pages and then opened the supplements. The gardening one was interesting. His garden needed a lot of work, but now was not the time of year to be outside weeding and such; besides he couldn't get down on his knees like he used to. Nonetheless, he put it aside for future reference.

He riffled through the pages and then saw an article relating to the history and origin of names. It seemed that many names were derived centuries ago, when people were named according to their occupation or profession. Butchers and tailors and so on. He wondered if his local butcher, Bert Lamb, had an ancestor who was in fact a butcher. And whether Mrs Inkpen, the lady who worked at the library, was related to an author or something. Horace pondered the origin of his own name Merryweather and whether in fact his ancestors lived somewhere where it was nice and warm and everyone was happy.

All this thinking was becoming tiring, and Horace let the newspaper drop from his hands as his eyelids started to droop and he nodded off.

Suddenly he was back to his childhood. It was a beautiful summer's day and he was on a beach playing with other children. The sand felt warm on his toes, and they were all building a sandcastle. He felt happy and wanted to stay there for ever. But then someone was calling his name and he turned to look back along the beach.

'I must go,' he said.

'Don't go, stay,' the children cried, but his name sounded louder and louder and Horace jerked awake with a start, aware that someone was banging on his door.

'Mr Merryweather, are you there?'

Horace got up with a bit of a stagger, made his way to the door and cautiously opened it. To his amazement, there was Mrs Thompson holding out a packet of biscuits.

She smiled at him. 'You left these behind,' she said.

He took the biscuits from her, rubbing his eyes with the other hand.

Horace remembered then, he had bought them, gingernuts, on the spur of the moment – something which he generally didn't do. How could he have forgotten? He tried to gather his thoughts ,which were still half at the beach.

'Thank you, Mrs Thompson. I must have nodded off. That is so kind of you. I'm sorry to give you so much trouble.' He was babbling a bit, flustered and quite unlike his usual self. Then to his surprise it just came out. 'Um…my name's Horace,' he said.

Mrs Thompson smiled, and started to turn round. 'I must get going,' she said, then turned back and looked at him. 'And I'm Ivy,' she said, then she gave a little wave as she made her way back to the van waiting at the kerb.

Horace closed the door in a bit of a daze. The heater was still going, and he felt nice and warm, like he had at the beach in his dream, so for a change Horace left it on for another half an hour.

He fetched a lamb chop from the fridge ready to cook for a late lunch and hummed to himself. Horace didn't usually hum, but for some unaccountable reason his spirits had lifted.

It would soon be spring, he thought, wouldn't it?

The Book

The book was on the seat where Brad was about to sit. He looked around to see if anyone else was going to sit down, but as there was no time to mess about looking and the train was getting ready to take off, he removed the book, sat down and held it in his lap.

There was another person sitting next to him by the window, an older man who was engrossed in his own book.

Brad gently nudged him, 'Excuse me,' he said politely.

The man turned to look at him a little annoyed that he had been disturbed. 'Yes?' he said.

'Somebody left this book behind. Did you notice who was sitting here?' He was aware, even as he spoke, that the person who had been sitting there was probably off the train by now anyway.

'No,' the man said, and turned away, not wishing to encourage any conversation.

So Brad looked at the book, realising that it wasn't your everyday book for reading, and it wasn't a magazine with pictures. It was small, about half the size of a small book, with a hard cover. It had flowers painted on it and in fancy lettering the words 'AUTOGRAPH BOOK'.

A little intrigued now, he opened it up and inside the front cover, and in the same fancy writing, were the words 'This book belongs to' and in careful childish writing was written 'Anthony Peabody', and the date 3 March 1980.

Brad turned the pages. On the first page someone had written 'By hook or by crook I'll be first in this book', and signed it 'Mary Parsons'.

Brad turned the following pages, numbered one to fifty. Some of them had been written on and signed by various people. One, who must have been Anthony's grandmother, had written, 'Your life lies all before you like a drift of pure white snow, be careful how you tread it, as all your footprints show.' It was signed 'Grandma Peabody'.

That's cool, thought Brad.

Then there were some drawings and poems. And Brad, who liked to draw, suddenly had an idea. He would make his mark. He opened his school backpack and found his coloured pencils, and choosing page number sixteen, which was just his age, he carefully drew a picture of his dog Bugsie, a brown and white mutt he had got from the lost dogs pound. He was pleased with his effort, and signed it 'Brad Taylor, 3 March, 2017'. Then, having a second thought, he wrote, 'PS Good Luck.'

It was getting close to his train stop by now, so Brad put everything away, and then wondered what to do with the book. He was not a stupid boy. He realised that this book was a bit different from other regular books and that he would like to have a better look through it. He debated, should he take it to the lost property office, or the police, or what? In the end, he packed it in with the rest of his school books and took it home.

Later that evening, he took it out along with his homework and put it on the desk in his room, where it stayed until one day when his mum Karen found it when she decided to clean his room.

'What's this, Brad? Who is Anthony Peabody?' she had turned the pages. '1980?' she said. 'Where did this come from?'

'I found it on the train,' he said. 'Somebody left it behind, and why are you looking through my stuff, Mum?, I need to know where everything is and now it's all disappeared.'

This conversation took place regularly, every time Karen decided to look for dirty washing and retrieve various dishes which belonged in the kitchen, so she didn't take much notice of her son's protestations, but this time it was a little different.

'This book obviously belongs to someone who has had it for a long time, thirty-seven years, in fact. Don't you think you should make an effort to find the owner? It's an autograph book, it's precious, and someone would have been devastated at losing it.'

'What's so special about an autograph book anyway? It's just an old book, and if it's so precious, then they should have taken better care of it.'

'Maybe so, but you don't know the circumstances. The person could have been taken ill or something and had to get off the train in a hurry.'

'OK, Mum, I get it, but how am I supposed to start looking?'

'Well, for starters, you could look in the phone book. Peabody isn't a very common name. You could make it a project. You could take it to school. Your teacher would be very impressed. Also, he'd know what an autograph book is. They don't print them so much any more, but a lot of people from my generation would all have had one at one time or another.'

So Brad, who had actually forgotten all about the book lying amongst the clutter on his desk, decided he would indeed try and find the owner. Truth be told, he liked a challenge and he also googled everything, so he booted the computer up and entered 'Anthony Peabody'.

Unfortunately, the only one he found was a musician in his twenties, who lived in America, so he went with his mother's idea and looked through the phone book. There were a few listed there, so he wrote them all down along with the numbers, but by then it was tea time so he put everything aside to do later. Of course, later, there was homework, and checking his phone for messages and a heap of other stuff that took priority over finding the owner of a (in his opinion) stupid old book.

But then, on the weekend, his mother reminded him again and so he started with the phone calls.

There were six Peabodys listed in his town and it took a while, because he had to explain every time and then wait while they asked other people. There were a couple of call backs after he had left a message, and some people had no idea what he was talking about.

'What about putting a notice in the lost and found column in the paper?' he asked his mum.

'Good idea, Brad,' she said and even offered to pay for it.

He was happy about that!

So a few days later the ad went in. 'Found on the 3.30 train from the city,' it said, 'an autograph book', and gave the telephone number to call.

For two days there was no response, and then on the third day someone rang.

'It's for you,' Brad's sister Bree said, and Brad, feeling quite important, because he never got calls on the landline, just text messages on his phone, said, 'Brad Taylor speaking.'

A young- sounding girl's voice said, 'Are you the one who found the autograph book?'

'Yes,' he said, 'that's right. Does it belong to you?'

'Er…no,' she said, 'not exactly, but I left it on the train.'

'You left it?'

'Yes.'

'Do you mean, on purpose?'

'Yes.'

'Why?'

'Because I found it on the seat and took it home, but then one day I decided to put it back where I found it.'

'Well,' said Brad a little self-righteously, 'I took its back home with me and now I'm trying to find the owner. So you don't know Anthony Peabody then do you?'

'No. I'm Emma Johnson. I wrote in it,' she said.

'You did? What page?'

'Page thirty-two.'

Brad grabbed the book which was on the telephone table, and quickly turned the pages. There she had written, 'Today is the first day of the rest of your life, Emma Johnson, 3 March 2016.'

'That's cool,' remarked Brad.

'Thanks. Well, I hope you find the owner. Just remember to look at the dates.' Then she was gone before Brad got a chance to ask her what she meant.

He was thumbing through the pages and suddenly noticed something he had missed before. Everyone who had written in the book had the same day and month but a different year.

He looked at Emma's page again. She had put '3 March 2016'. He looked back at Grandma Peabody's '3 March 1980', the same day that Anthony Peabody had written his name.

This was getting all a bit weird for Brad, so he got a pen and paper and carefully went through the whole book, writing down all the dates on the different page numbers until he had a list.

Every year since 1980 there was a page written on 3 March on a different year until this year, 2017. This had happened for thirty-seven years, which meant there were thirteen blank pages left, making fifty altogether. He counted them to make sure, then went and showed it to his mum, who was a bit freaked out, but it was obvious what he had to do.

Brad kept the book for the rest of the year, and then on the 3 March 2018 he caught the same train home from town like he always did, and when he reached the station, he left the book on the seat. He didn't know who would be sitting there, but it had worked in the past and he had to trust to luck that it would work in the future, for the next thirteen years anyway.

Brad was a smart kid. One day, he googled '3 March' to see if anything had happened on that day in 1980, and there it was: a collision between two trains, due to malfunction of signals. Fifty people were injured or killed. On the list of passengers who were killed was Anthony Peabody, who had just had his tenth birthday, and Else Peabody, aged sixty-two.

Henry's Fifteen Minutes of Fame

A single beam of light shone on the centre of the stage. The audience were getting restless, muttering amongst themselves. Then someone started a slow clap. One of the judges in front of the stage rose to her feet, looked around then sat down again and said something to one of the other judges.

Then the spotlight suddenly shifted from the middle of the stage to the right-hand side. The audience quietened, and all the heads moved as one, like clowns, waiting for the ball to drop. Expectant, wondering, curious now as to what had caused the hold-up, ready to make judgements on the perceived tardiness of the next act. The judges stopped talking to one another and settled back in their seats.

An elderly gentleman emerged, shuffling slowly along from behind the curtain. He was on the short side, quite plump and wearing a black shiny suit which was probably borrowed, as it was a little bit short in the arms and legs. His shoes were also shiny, well polished, and he wore a red bow tie. An old-fashioned bowler hat came low down over his eyes, so that you couldn't see whether he had any hair. All in all, he presented an odd sort of appearance for a contestant on a talent show.

One of the judges glanced at the others and rolled her eyes, sighing, and one of the them started to shuffle papers, showing little interest in this next uninspiring-looking contestant who was blinking up at the spotlight shielding his eyes.

Then the compère was introducing him. 'This is Henry Watson,' he informed the audience. 'He is going to sing for us.' He bent towards Henry. 'What are you going to sing?' He placed an arm around the old fellow's shoulder, seeking perhaps to give him courage.

'"Nessun Dorma".' Henry's voice was a little quavery.

'Off you go then. Good luck.' The compère gave him a pat on the back and drew away. The spotlight seemed to brighten as it settled over the insignificant figure of Henry Watson as he prepared for his fifteen minutes of fame, along with all the other hopefuls making their debut this night.

He waited, looking anxiously towards the wings. It seemed an age before the music started, although it was probably only a few seconds. Then Henry straightened up, seeming to gain height, gathered himself together, closed his eyes, took a deep breath and began to sing.

The audience hushed and there was silence throughout the auditorium as his voice gained power and began to soar with a purity and depth completely unexpected from this unassuming old gentleman. The judges looked at one another in amazement, and tears started from the same eyes of the judge which had been rolling before.

As the last notes died away, Henry looked around, a dazed expression on his face as though emerging from a dream. There was a moment's silence before the audience erupted with a roar. They were standing up, cheering and clapping, as were the judges.

The compère emerged again, looking very impressed. He grasped Henry's hand. 'That was totally awesome,' he said, and gently turned him to face the judges.

One of them was raising his hand to quieten the audience.

For Henry, the next few minutes were a blur. They wanted to know where he had learnt to sing. He told them he hadn't and that he had just always sang for the customers in his barber's shop. And no, he had never performed in public like this before. He nodded and smiled and wished they would hurry up. His feet were hurting in the tight shoes and he wanted to get off the stage.

'We'd like you to come back for the finals,' they said.

Henry gave a little bow and doffed his hat, revealing a mass of thick grey hair. 'Thank you.' he said politely, then shuffled off the stage.

'What a find,' remarked a judge excitedly. 'I think we have a potential winner there.' He turned to the others, 'OK, who's next?'

Henry had already made up his mind. He knew he wouldn't be coming back, what with all the stress, and having to dress up, and putting up with all the stupid questions from those people. He greeted his two mates waiting in the wings, who had dobbed him in for this in the first place.

'Well, I'm glad that's over,' he said as they hugged and patted him on the back.

So he didn't go back. Sometimes Henry thought of how it would have been to be in the spotlight again and listen to all those people clapping and cheering. But it wasn't for him. He had had his fifteen minutes of fame and that was enough.

What Henry didn't anticipate, though, was the fact that it had all been televised. His barber's shop became inundated with customers needing haircuts and he had to employ another barber. So business boomed, Henry kept singing and, without him quite realising it, he became rather famous.

Valentine's Day

The florist shop had almost sold out. Valentine's Day was the busiest of the year and Priscilla always made sure that she went to the market early to get a good assortment of flowers and plants for her stock. There had been baskets and bouquets to prepare and she had had to organise an extra delivery person to make sure that all her orders were delivered in good time.

They were all done now. Priscilla sat down with a tired sigh and looked around her shop. There weren't many flowers left, which was good. It meant that she had made enough profit on sales to see her through the coming week, to pay the bills and her two staff members. They had worked tirelessly since early morning.

'Thanks, girls,' she had told them. 'I appreciate all your work today. Now go home. I'll see you tomorrow.'

It had been a hard battle. When she bought the shop, it was a run-down grocery store which had closed because of the emergence of a nearby supermarket. But she had looked around the area and decided that it definitely needed a florist, and she was an aspiring florist who needed a shop. She had also decided that it was time she started working for herself instead of watching someone else taking the credit for her ideas. She knew where the best markets were, she had been driver, sales person and general factotum, and had learned a lot about the business. She knew how to make it work. It had been a bit of a gamble and a struggle at first. But she had started small and only bought what she thought would sell. Gradually customers came, and as her stock grew so did her clients. PRISCILLA BLOOMS in large fancy lettering had been firmly attached over the front window and Priscilla finally had an up and coming business that was beginning to be firmly established.

She lived in the tiny flat over the shop and there was a car park around the back with an outside staircase she used when the shop was closed.

Priscilla was gracious and helpful to her customers. She always took great care of her appearance and carefully applied make-up. The long colourful skirts, peasant-style blouses, shoulder-length blonde wavy hair and sweet smile fitted perfectly with the old world ambience she strived to cultivate. She spoke quietly and always gave each customer her full attention, making suggestions and offering advice on floral selections.

There was always soft background music playing, and seats where customers could discuss bridal flowers or funeral wreaths without feeling pressured.

She glanced towards the back of the shop where there was a partition shielding a corner with a small sign saying 'Make your own bunch for $10'. There were always a few odds and ends, discarded and left-over flowers from bouquets, or some a little bit wilted but still good enough to last for a few days, and it was better, she thought, to sell them cheaply than throw them out.

A customer was there rifling through them. He was a regular: Jim Baxter. He came every week. Sometimes Priscilla wondered who the flowers were for, but he never said. He always stayed for a chat and seemed to make excuses to stay longer than was necessary. He generally wore a suit and she thought maybe he was in business of some kind, but she never liked to pry. She wished now that he would hurry up and go, as she needed to close the shop.

She had taken in all the flowers which had been outside in the cart. People were leaving town in a hurry to catch their trains or buses, the window shoppers were gone and the street was fairly quiet.

Priscilla looked out of the shop window and frowned as she saw a scruffy-looking man in a tracksuit peering through the window. She had a feeling about people and she didn't much like the look of this one.

She went to the door as he approached. 'I'm sorry, I'm about to close,' she said politely.

He roughly pushed her aside and strode into the shop.

Priscilla stood still, not appearing to offer any resistance. She glanced out of the window. There were always two of them, she thought, and sure enough, there was another one, who looked like this one's brother, pacing up and down outside.

'OK, lady.' The thug pulled out a knife and waved it front of her face then dragged a plastic bag out of his pocket. 'I'll have the cash from the till. Make it quick and don't make a fuss, then you won't get hurt,'

For a moment, Priscilla didn't do anything, Then quickly, before he had time to react, she executed two clean blows, one to his wrist with such a force that he dropped the knife, and a punch to his midriff which sent him sprawling onto the floor. She grabbed his tracksuit front and dragged him back up, while kicking the knife out of reach, then quickly put him in a headlock.

'If I see your face in here again,' she told him in a voice that had changed to a fearsome snarl, 'I'll break your head, do you understand?!'

His eyes were watering as she loosened her grip, and he managed a weak nod.

'Now get out of here.' She opened the door, gave him a hefty push and he landed on his hands and knees outside. Then she watched as he grabbed his brother and they both fled up the street.

Priscilla sighed and was about to pull the blinds down when she remembered Jim Baxter. She glanced around and there he was, eyes as big as saucers; he couldn't believe what he had just seen. He came forward with a bunch of flowers and money in his hand, which was shaking a little bit, but she waved him past. 'It's on the house, Jim,' she told him. 'Happy Valentines Day.'

'Thank you,' he murmured and, eyes averted, quickly hurried out.

Priscilla finished closing up the shop and, as she collected money from the till, noticed an envelope on the counter which hadn't been there before. She opened it up to discover a beautiful Valentines card. 'From a secret admirer', it said.

'Oh, my…Jim Parsons.' she murmured. She knew it couldn't have been anyone else.

Upstairs in her flat, Priscilla went into the bedroom, where she removed the blonde wig and placed it on a stand alongside another very similar one. She dropped her skirt on to the floor, revealing strong hairy legs. She pulled off her blouse and kicked off her shoes then made for the shower, emerging a few minutes later wearing jeans and a T-shirt, the short dark hair still wet.

Bruce could relax and be himself for a while. It would be an early start in the morning to catch the best bargains at the market.

He took out a frozen dinner from the fridge and put it in the microwave, turned on the TV and relaxed in his armchair.

Then he reached for the Valentines card. 'Sorry, Jim,' he said. He had a feeling Jim wouldn't be back.

Frogs

'They'll be drinks and snacks.' Patty was trying to persuade her friend Julia to go to the book launch.

'But I'm not really interested,' Julia told her, 'plus I don't want any more books. Who is it, anyway, and what kind of book is it?'

'I'm not really sure,' Patty said. 'It's just to support my friend Jeremy really, plus the launch is at the gallery. I think it's to do with the secret life of frogs or something. You like going to the gallery, don't you? Come on, Julia. I don't want to go by myself.'

'Frogs? You've got to be kidding, Patty. I hate frogs. Who would want to write about frogs?'

'Well, it's Jeremy's first book, and he'll sign it for you if you buy one, and that'll be worth something if he gets famous one day. He's really into research and science and stuff. Come on, Julia, you can always look at some pictures if you get bored.'

So Julia gave in. 'OK, she said, 'I'll come, just so you'll stop nagging me.'

They went along to the gallery, where, much to Julia's disgust, they were showing pictures of frogs, big ones, small ones, colourful ones.

'You've got to be kidding!' she exclaimed, as she looked around. 'There's nothing but frogs.'

Patty smiled as they joined the other book launching people and were handed a glass of wine. 'Well, it's a book about frogs, so I suppose they decided to back it up with some frog pictures. Anyway, some of these are gorgeous. I didn't know there were so many different colours. I think they're fantastic.'

Julia looked disbelievingly at her friend, and turned round as she noticed a man coming towards her.

'Hi.' He held out his hand and she automatically responded as he wrapped it around hers.

'Julia, isn't it?' he asked.

She nodded, taking note of the muscled frame, the thick dark hair and nice brown eyes. 'Do I know you?' she asked him, then looked at Patty, who was murmuring excuses as she suddenly disappeared into the crowd.

'I'm Jeremy,' he smiled. 'You're a friend of Patty's, aren't you? I saw you at Jake's birthday party, but never got a chance to introduce myself, which I'm taking the opportunity do now,' he added.

Julia was momentarily stuck dumb, which for her was unusua,l to say the least. 'Is this your book launch then?' she asked, suddenly twigging what sneaky Patty was up to. But suddenly she didn't mind. Her match-making friend might have got it right for once. She regarded Jeremy with interest.

'Yes,' he said. 'Are you interested in frogs? Absolutely amazing little creatures, aren't they?'

'Oh, absolutely, yes indeed,' Julia replied enthusiastically. 'I love frogs. I intend to buy one of your books.'

'Well, thank you,' Jeremy beamed at her. He took her arm and guided her towards the food table. 'How about some drinks and snacks?'

Time to Sing

When the vacancy had come up unexpectedly in the retirement village and was offered to Percy, he realised it was time to make a decision. He had been thinking about selling the big family home for a long time now, ever since Dora had passed away, but hadn't quite been able to do it. There were a lot of memories tied up in the old place, but in the end common sense prevailed, together with his daughter's urging.

'There's hardly ever a vacancy there and you might not get the chance again for ages. So do it, Dad. We'll all help with everything.'

So in the end he had given in. The house had sold quickly because it was close to the beach. His family had all chipped in to help with the moving and disposal of unwanted furniture and so on, and it had all happened so quickly that Percy was still feeling uprooted, homesick for the old place and unsettled.

His unit had been freshly painted, and there was a well equipped kitchen. He had the choice of eating in the cafeteria, or cooking for himself. Percy liked to cook, so he had been eating at home. The shops were within walking distance and he was happy to discover a good well stocked library within the village.

But still he hadn't been able to join in with any of the activities. There were plenty to choose from" Snooker or table tennis in the community hall, swimming in the pool, live concerts, bus trips. The options were endless. There was even a bowling green. But nothing appealed to Percy. He was fine, he told himself. Indeed, he thought he was. He had his DVDs, CDs, books and TV – plenty of things to keep him occupied.

One night he picked up the picture of Dora that he kept on the bedside table. 'Well, old girl.' he murmured, gently touching the face of an elderly lady with white curly hair and a sweet smile, 'I've done it. I've left the old place. It's been sold and I've moved into a nice little unit. I think you'd like it here. There's plenty to do, and lots of people to meet. Not that I'm much interested,' he sighed. 'I miss having a shed to potter in, and I've got no garden to speak of, just paving and lots of pots.'

One morning there was a knock on his door and Percy was surprised to see his next-door neighbour Stan. He had met Stan the day he had moved in. He had introduced himself, they had shaken hands and Stan had welcomed him to the neighbourhood. Percy hadn't heard or seen anyone else next door, so assumed that his neighbour was living on his own. He had thought about inviting him around for a drink but so far hadn't got around to it.

'Hi, Stan, come in.' Percy stepped aside as a tall bearded man walked past him into the lounge room.

'How're you settling in?' Stan looked around, smiled. 'Looks good.'

'Thanks, yes, I guess I'm settling in OK. Would you like a coffee – or a beer?'

Stan shook his head. 'No thanks, I'm good. I just called for a quick chat.'

'Yes?' Percy was curious.

'Well,' Stan hesitated, 'I was wondering.'

Percy nodded encouragingly, eyebrows raised.

'Well, see, they, that is the committee who looks after activities in the village, are looking for people to start up a choir. There are plenty of ladies, but they need more blokes. Tenors and basses,' Stan told him. 'I'm thinking about joining, I'm not a joiner of things usually, but thought I might give it a go. So I was wondering if you might be interested.'

Stan was looking anxiously at him, and Percy could say nothing for a long moment.

'Well,' he said slowly, 'I don't know. I don't know if I could do it. It's been a few good years since I was in a choir.'

He was remembering about his school years. He had been in the high school choir, and had a good tenor voice in those days. Then there had been the church choir until life caught up, and going to church slowly became part of his past.

For the first time in a long time, Percy felt a twinge of excitement.

Stan beamed. 'Then you'll think about it? The first practice night is Wednesday in the community hall. I'd appreciate your company,' he added.

Percy nodded. He couldn't believe he was actually agreeing to this. 'I'll think about it,' he said.

So he did. He put some music on and sang along. His voice was rusty, a bit crackly, but maybe it would come good with a bit of practice, he thought.

It was with a little nervousness, mixed with excited anticipation, that Percy and Stan fronted up at the community hall the next Wednesday night. Percy decided to wear a new blue shirt that had been waiting for the right occasion, and had donned his red baseball cap to cover his balding pate. He noticed that Stan had trimmed his rather straggly grey beard and looked quite spruce.

They looked around at about twenty other people, self-consciously shuffling their feet and looking at a lady who introduced herself as Freda Batty, a retired music teacher, who explained about the choir which she hoped to put together with this bunch of retirees – most of whom hadn't sung for years.

She thanked them all for coming. 'And don't worry if you can't read music,' she told them. 'We're going to do songs that you're sure to know to start with, and you'll soon pick it up. It'll be Christmas in a couple of months,' she added, 'so we're going to learn some carols.'

She was confident, reassuring. People were starting to relax. Sheets of music were handed out and everyone was sorted into their groups of sopranos, altos, tenors and basses.

Percy and Stan were two of the four tenors and there were three basses. The rest were women not sure of where they should go, so it was a bit of a shambles for a while. But eventually they were all settled and in their places. An efficient-looking lady pianist sat down at the piano and then they got started.

The first song was a bit shaky, but then they all got into it. Self-consciousness was disappearing. Some people got into their parts straight away and Percy's pure tenor voice gradually strengthened as he easily followed the music. He realised he was actually enjoying himself. He glanced sideways at Stan, who was singing with gusto, and a feeling of great joy washed over Percy with an exhilaration of spirit he had quite forgotten he ever knew.

When they were finished for the evening, there was plenty of happy chatter and Freda was beaming at them all.

'Well done, everyone,' she said, 'and hopefully I'll see you all again next week.'

Someone stood up and thanked her for a great evening and everyone spontaneously clapped.

That night, Percy was still on a high and he couldn't settle to sleep. He picked up Dora's picture. 'Guess what,' he told her. 'I've joined a choir.'

It seemed like her smile broadened just a little, as though she was about to laugh, but it may have been because he had taken his glasses off and everything was a bit blurry.

Afterwards

The battle was over, the guns silent at last, and the villagers who had been caught trying to escape lay on the ground where they had fallen. The faint moans of those who hadn't been killed outright gradually ceased.

The victors departed in their trucks, laughing, as they surveyed the carnage they had caused. There had been no spies hiding there, and even if there had been, nobody would have given them up, so they all paid the price.

In their haste to leave, the soldiers didn't notice that they had left behind one of their own. A young conscripted recruit, who had hidden at the back of one of the ramshackle huts, not wanting to take part in the deadly executions of villagers whose meagre supply of guns was not nearly enough to withstand the ferocious onslaught. The young soldier knew he would be shot if they had found him. He had to get as far away from this place as soon as possible, knowing that as soon as they realised he was absent, they would come back looking for him.

Suddenly he stiffened. There was a movement behind the next hut, and he drew back into the shadows, holding his breath as a big cardboard box began to move. Then it tipped over and crawling out from underneath emerged a small child, probably only three or four years old. He was ragged and dirty and stood up unsteadily, holding his hand to his head, which was bleeding.

As the soldier watched, the boy tottered towards the body of a woman lying on the ground close by. He bent down and began patting her face for a while talking to her, then gave a great cry of anguish when he couldn't make her stir.

The young soldier watched in pity, and tears filled his eyes. He struggled to his feet. His leg was bleeding; he had fallen onto a rock in his haste to hide from the fighting.

The child turned and saw him and held out his arms, looking for comfort from another human while he cried for his mother.

So the young soldier picked up the boy and hugged him, giving as much comfort as he could, and in return received the trust of a child who didn't recognise him as the enemy. He dipped his handkerchief into a bucket of water standing near the well, and gently cleaned the boy's face, then attended to his own cut knee bleeding through torn trousers.

He rocked the child, who soon fell into an exhausted sleep, then carefully laid him on the ground. Next he searched the huts, and returned dressed in the simple jacket and trousers that had belonged to one of the villagers.

He had hidden his uniform underneath a pile of rubbish, found some rice and fish which he stuffed into a sack, then returned to the boy, who was awake now and greeted the soldier with a little smile.

There was no more time to waste, so he hoisted the child onto his back, threw the sack of food over his shoulder, and started the long walk away from the carnage and sounds of distant gunfire.

The child clung tightly to his back at first and the soldier could feel him shaking, but gradually the boy relaxed and fell asleep.

The young soldier smiled then, picked up his pace and softly began singing a folk song.

The Empty Chair

He stopped at the doorway and regarded the half dozen or so residents in their armchairs, gathered around in a half circle in front of a big TV. They all appeared to be dozing; one lady was gentle snoring. No one seemed to be actually watching the TV and he wondered whether anyone would notice if he went over and tuned it onto the footy. There was a vacant chair and he eyed it, ready to make his move.

He crept slowly forward into the room and looked around for a remote control on the nearby table, but couldn't see one. He was about to switch the channel over by hand when he heard a loud thump and someone's voice voice boomed, 'Leave it alone, I'm watching that!'

He jumped and turned around to see an elderly gentleman with whiskers, banging his stick on the floor and pointing at the screen.

'Sorry,' he said, and turned around to leave. He didn't want to cause any trouble.

'Are you new, then?' Another voice same from the depths of another chair and he turned to face the woman who had been snoring.

'Yes,' he said.

'Well, you can't sit in that chair, that's Harry's. He isn't here today but it's his for when he comes.'

'Oh, OK then,' he said. 'I'll go and find another one.'

But he didn't. He went back to his room and sat in the chair there. It wasn't very comfortable. He wished he had organised a TV for his room before moving in but it had all happened so quickly, there hadn't been time.

He opened his suitcase, which he had stored in the top of the wardrobe, and got out an old *Reader's Digest* he had found on the bus he'd taken to get here and settled down to read until lunchtime.

He found the dining room on his floor where he had been told to go and was directed to a table for four with an empty chair. The three people who were already seated leant toward one another as soon as they saw him coming and conversed in whispers. He recognised one of them from the TV room.

'What about Harry?' he heard a woman say. 'What about when he comes back? Where is he going to go? He always sits with us.'

He was ignored throughout the meal and suspicious glances were cast in his direction at regular intervals, so he finished his meal as quickly as he could and returned to his room.

He lay on his bed for a while, dozing, then got up and made a cup of tea. At least there was a kettle and some sugar, tea and coffee bags, and a small bottle of milk in the mini fridge, plus two mugs. He had a packet of biscuits in his bag as well.

The silence was overwhelming. There were no traffic noises, yelling children, or thumping music. Sometimes he could hear people talking quietly outside his door, and he waited for a knock, but they passed along, leaving him once again to the quiet, his thoughts and his book. He wondered if there was a library and decided that tomorrow he would have a proper look around.

He didn't go to the dining room for dinner that night. He made do with the rest of the biscuits and cups of tea. He wasn't hungry anyway, he thought, and if Harry comes back wanting his chair, then there could be a problem.

He didn't want to be a nuisance, so he went to bed early, waking at daylight feeling very hungry. He showered and dressed, then waited until it was time for breakfast, which started at 7.30.

He was the first to arrive and was pleased to find that there was no one else at his table. He enjoyed the eggs, bacon and toast and was about to leave just as the others arrived. He smiled at them as they passed.

He went back to his room for a little while and then decided to go for a look round. He went down in the lift to the outside area and found a community garden, with benches and shrubs. It was pleasant there. He sat for a while and watched the birds and, surprisingly, a possum, which appeared for a brief moment before disappearing again.

There seemed to be very few people about and no one took any notice of him. He was looking for someone to ask where the games room was, but the nurses all seemed to be busy rushing about, and he saw no one that looked like they could be one of the residents.

They had told him when he had arrived that there was a games room and he also wanted to find out if there was a library. But he lacked the courage to stop anyone to ask, so in the end he started walking around the corridors until he found the lift again and then went up.

When he got out, though, everything looked different. The walls of the corridor were painted yellow. His floor was blue – he remembered that, blue being his favourite colour – but he couldn't remember which number floor it was. He realised he was lost. He needed to find his room now; the all too familiar stirrings of panic were starting up and his heart began racing.

He was standing in front of the lift, wondering what to do when it opened and a nurse stepped out.

She looked in his eyes saw his agitation. 'Hello,' she smiled. 'Are you lost?'

'Yes, I can't find my room,' he said.

She bent forward and looked closely at his identification tag in its plastic case which he had remembered to pin to his shirt. 'Oh, yes, number 38. That's the next floor down,' she told him. 'Follow me, Bert, and I'll see you back.'

So they got into the lift, down a floor and then around corridors until with relief he saw his door number.

'Thank you,' he said, and then she waited while he found the key in his pocket and put it into the lock.

He turned to her. 'It's very quiet,' he remarked. 'Not many people here, are there?'

'Oh well,' she said. 'They're probably all at Harry's funeral. Take care now, Bert,' she added, then patted his arm, turned and left.

He thought for a moment, then locked the door again. and went to the TV room which was close by. There was no one there now, so he turned the TV on and sat in Harry's chair, which was quite comfortable, and in a little while nodded off.

He jerked awake, though, when he realised people were talking close by.

'Looks like Harry's not coming back, then,' a woman's voice said.

He felt a nudge on his shoulder.

'What's your name then?' she asked.

He looked up her. 'Bert.'

'Well,' she said, 'looks like you can have Harry's chair, then.'

'Thank you,' he said.

She pulled a remote control out of her pocket and changed the programme to the cricket. 'Harry never liked the football,' she said. 'He only liked the cricket.'

'I like cricket as well,' he said.

Then suddenly they all relaxed and sat down in their armchairs. They smiled at him.

'Where are you from, then?' someone asked.

So Bert relaxed as well. He didn't think it would ever happen to him but it seemed he was one of them now, so he supposed he had better make the best of it.

He settled back in his armchair and started telling them his story,

Images

Annabel looked closely at the painting. It was one of those trick scenes where a person looked into a mirror to see her own reflection of herself looking into a mirror. Each picture got smaller and smaller until it finally vanished into the distance. She counted six heads of an elderly lady with white hair drawn back into a bun and wearing a white frilly blouse with a beautiful cameo brooch on the front and a little smile as though she had just heard an amusing joke. Annabel wondered whether she was some family member, or just someone from the artist's imagination.

She had only just started this job. The advertisement had been in the local post office window. 'Temporary cleaner required', it said, and underneath was a telephone number on a little tear-off slip. She had never done cleaning for a job before, but what the heck, she thought, how hard can it be? She needed some extra cash if she was going to be able to finish her degree. She was just about scraping by at the moment. It was cheap staying at the uni campus but her student allowance didn't allow for any extras.

So she had applied for the job, had an interview at an office in town with an agent, a businesslike female in a black suit, who said she was acting on behalf of a Mrs Barker-Jones, the owner of the residence where Annabel would be working, and then discussed what duties would be required of her and the type of work that needed to be done. They decided upon four hours on Wednesday mornings, when Annabel didn't have a class, and six hours on Saturdays, for one month. Her job, it seemed, would be mainly vacuuming, dusting and polishing, and any other jobs that her employer required her to do.

The following Wednesday morning, Annabel had had arrived early.

She had allowed enough time to find the residence as it was well outside of town. It was accessed by a long winding driveway almost covered by overhanging trees and she gasped when the very old mansion came into view; it was enormous. She checked the address again to make sure she was at the right place before pulling the old-fashioned bell.

The elderly gentleman who opened the door scrutinised her carefully before holding out his hand. 'How do you do, Miss Wellington,' he said in a gravelly formal voice.

Annabel gave her best winning smile, 'How do you do,' she answered.

He stepped back, holding the door open for her. 'I am Mr Forbes. I will show you where the cleaning equipment is,' he said, and then turned and started walking away. 'Please follow me, and I will explain your duties.'

So, somewhat bemused, Annabel followed him through corridors until they came to an enormous kitchen leading to a utility room at the back, where she regarded the vacuum cleaner, polisher, mops, buckets, brushes and all the other cleaning apparatus. She had a moment's panic: the house was so big; how was she going to cope with this lot?

'Mr Forbes was speaking again. 'Today you will dust the artefacts and polish the ground floor,' he said, indicating the floor polisher. 'On Saturday you will vacuum the stairs and the carpets on the upper floor.' He regarded her carefully. 'Are you going to manage that?' he asked.

Annabel nodded. 'No worries,' she said brightly. 'That's fine. Um,' she hesitated, 'when do I get to meet Mrs Barker-Jones?'

'At the moment, Mrs Barker-Jones is indisposed,' he said. 'Later on you may meet her. You just need to do your work and there will be no problems.'

So she had set off with polish, floor polisher and dusters.

The old mansion had original paintings on all the walls, antique furniture, a well stocked library, dining and drawing rooms. Upstairs there were apparently many bedrooms and bathrooms. Annabel thought she would get around to counting them all sometime. She had stopped to admire the paintings, which was why she was so intrigued by the one with the lady and the mirrors.

She looked at her watch. Two hours had passed by already. There were another two to go and she still hadn't finished the polishing, so she moved along quickly, taking time to apply polish to a beautiful old grand piano, wondering if she dare play a tune on it. Too risky, she thought; better not chance getting fired on my first day. She sighed and carried on with her dusting and polishing.

Mr Forbes appeared suddenly just as she was retuning the cleaning equipment to the utility room. 'You seem to have done very well, Miss Wellington,' he said.

He must have been checking up on me, Annabel thought.

'You may go now,' he continued. 'I'll expect you on Saturday.' He pointed to a door which led outside. 'In future when you come, you may use this door and get to work as soon as you arrive. Payment will be made on Saturday. Good afternoon, Miss Wellington.' With that, he disappeared back through the kitchen, leaving her to find her own way out.

Once outside, she took deep breaths of the fresh air. It had been stuffy inside the old house. In spite of the big rooms and high ceilings, there had been a pervasive air of age, mustiness and gloom. She wondered when she would get to get to see the owner, and who did the cooking: was Mr Forbes the cook or was he the butler? It was all a bit creepy, she decided, then put it all out of her mind for now. She had study to do for tomorrow and a thesis to work on.

On Saturday, Annabel found her way to the back of the house and in through the rear door, which was unlocked, to the utility room. She put on an apron which she had brought with her this time, and dragged the vacuum cleaner out through the kitchen into the hallway and started on the carpets. There seemed to be no one about, but nevertheless she had a feeling of being watched and glanced around a few times. Just my imagination, she decided, as she emptied the dust bag out for the second time. No wonder this place smelt musty, she thought; I wonder when it was vacuumed last.

She stopped alongside the painting of the mirror lady to have another look. Then peered closer. Something was different. She counted the heads: five. She was sure there were six when she first saw it. Annabel frowned. She must have been wrong; this was a bit weird! But she couldn't have been wrong, she thought; she remembered counting them at least twice. Perhaps there were two pictures.

Annabel continued with her work, looking out for other similar paintings. She had to get going and not waste any more time, and dragged the vacuum up the stairs, cleaning the stair carpet as she went.

It was cold upstairs. The passages and the bedrooms were all carpeted. Only four rooms had furniture, old-fashioned four-poster beds and antique dressers. Three rooms were empty apart from one room which had a child's rocking horse and a big box of toys. The remaining door was locked.

Annabel stopped and pondered. Was Mrs Barker-Jones in there? If not, then where ? She put her ear close to the door; nothing but silence, so she bent down to look through the keyhole but it was blocked by the key from the other side.

She checked all the other doors again. A linen cupboard, three bathrooms and a small sitting room. No more bedrooms. She looked again to see if there were any other stairs going up to another floor; no luck there either

Annabel decided it was time to find Mr Forbes. She had questions. She was beginning to feel spooked about the whole thing, and looked at her watch. Time for lunch. So she left the vacuum where it was and headed back downstairs to the utility room.

She picked up an envelope sitting on top of her lunch box, which she had left on a small table. 'MISS WELLINGTON' was written on the front in large block letters followed by the words, 'This is your payment for 10 hours work.' Inside was $200.

Annabel smiled and stuffed the notes inside her wallet. Mr Forbes obviously trusted her to finish her work today, so that's what she'd do, she decided. She'd seen no sign of him, but what the heck, she thought, I'm getting paid; the rest of it was none of her business.

She took her lunch outside. It was warm in the sun and she sat on a seat by a little fountain, then wandered around the well kept grounds. She wondered where the gardener was. There had to be a gardener, she thought, to look after all this.

The first thing Annabel did when she arrived the following Wednesday was to look at the strange painting, just to set her mind at rest.

She stood very still in front of it as a cold shiver passed through body; her heart seemed to stop for a moment as Annabel counted four heads and mirrors. The front one was a little further back. The two at the rear had been replaced with what looked like part of the garden. She could see the side of a water fountain just to the left.

Annabel was feeling really spooked by now. She contemplated walking away right there and then but remembered her pay packet. She needed the money. There had been a note left for her again. 'Today you will polish all the upstairs furniture', it said. So, gathering herself together, Annabel got on with it and at the end of four hours she tidied everything away and let herself out.

When Saturday came round again, she hoped Mr Forbes would appear but there was no sign of him and, as before, a note had been left for her. It was the all the bathrooms that had to be cleaned this time. Three upstairs and one next to the utility room which just had a shower and a toilet. The tiles on all of them were in a terrible state, so Annabel found brushes, a bucket and cleaning stuff and set off to start work.

She had decided to ignore the painting today, it was all too weird, but even so, curiosity won out and she found herself looking for it as she walked along the passage, even though she could hardly bear to look, and dreaded finding out if anything else had happened.

But sure enough it had changed again. Three heads this time. The water fountain was in full view now; the head of the lady was further back into the picture.

There was no sign of Mr Forbes, so she had no choice but to get on with the work if she was to get paid. The lunchtime envelope was there again, though, so she happily pocketed the cash. And spent the afternoon mostly on her knees cleaning the bathrooms.

The two faces which appeared the following Wednesday were just that of the lady looking at herself reflected in one mirror. She was sitting on a bench in the garden near the fountain and with a jolt Annabel realised it was the same bench she usually sat on when she had her lunch.

So, rather intrigued now as well as still feeling a little spooked, she arrived on Saturday wondering what would happen next. Her month would be up next Wednesday. She still hadn't heard or seen any sign of Mrs Barker-Jones. Perhaps she wasn't here at all, Annabel decided; perhaps she was in a nursing home Of course, that was it. And Mr Forbes was only the caretaker Perhaps they were getting the place cleaned up to sell it. With these comforting thoughts in mind, she read the note which had been left for her with instructions to go through the house again, making sure everything was dusted and clean.

When she looked at the picture again, Annabel wasn't too surprised to find that the lady with the mirror was on her own. You could only see her back, and her reflection was very indistinct, as though the paintbrush had slipped and blurred it all.

At lunchtime that day, her pay envelope was there as usual, but this time as well as the cash there was something wrapped in tissue paper nestling in the corner. Mystified, Annabel unwrapped it and found a beautiful cameo brooch. Plus a little note. 'Thank you for your service it read. Your last day will be next Wednesday.'

'Wow,' she breathed. 'How about that!' and she pinned it to the lapel of her denim shirt. Cool, she thought, and gave a little joyous jig. 'Who'da thought?'

That afternoon, she went through the house again, making sure everything was clean and sparkling. She even stopped at the grand piano and played a little tune she'd remembered from her music lessons.

Annabel finished up that day and almost decided not to go back – after all, it looked as though her work was done – but when the next Wednesday came round, curiosity got the better of her and she arrived wondering what she would have to do.

There were no instructions waiting for her this time, so she wandered through the house, noticing with surprise that the floors were looking quite dirty again already, and ending up of course at the painting.

This time, though, Annabel was so horrified, she almost passed out. The painting had been restored to the image of six faces looking into mirrors, but the face wasn't that of an elderly lady, it was hers! Annabel looked at herself looking into a mirror six times, wearing on the lapel of her blue shirt the cameo she had been given.

She started to turn round, still in shock, as she sensed rather than saw someone coming up behind her…

A week later, Margery Johnson, recently widowed and looking to earn some extra cash, was reading a notice in the local post office window. 'Temporary cleaner required', it said, and underneath was a telephone number on a little tear-off slip.

Chance

It looked like a pile of rubbish that someone had tipped out of their car: bottles, cans, half empty cartons of food, cigarette butts, plastic bags, and a T-shirt with large stains which could have been anything but looked suspiciously like blood. Or so Jackson thought as he gazed at the mess in disgust.

He had stopped to check the water and was lifting the hood when he had glanced sideways and noticed the pile of rubbish which had been dumped under a tree at the side of the road.

It was isolated here on this part of the highway. Only one car had passed him in the last ten minutes. There had been a sign way back reading a hundred ks to the next rest stop and he had been hoping to get there before dark, but he couldn't take the risk of overheating and always carried spare water in case. Better to be safe than sorry, he thought. He had to deliver the old Holden in one piece to a vintage car collector, and then pick up another vehicle to drive back home.

He finished checking the oil and water and slammed down the hood. Something in his peripheral vision caught his eye as he glanced at the heap of rubbish again. He thought he had seen something move. He shook his head. Seeing things, he thought, but looked closer anyway.

The T-shirt moved. This time there had been no mistake. Cautiously he stepped towards it. It could be a snake and if it was then there was no way he was going near it. But perhaps it was an animal, a rat or a possum maybe. He thought for a moment; perhaps he should just leave it alone and get going.

He was about to open the car door again when curiosity got the better of him. He picked up a long piece of fallen tree branch, then stepped back to the pile of rubbish and gently prodded the shirt, standing as far away as he could; ready to make a run for it.

But whatever it was, it went completely still. So he prodded a bit harder, pushing a little bit. This time, the movement of the thing was sudden. Still covered by the T-shirt, it made for the bushes. It looked weird and funny at the same time and Jackson started to laugh. He was reminded of a game they played as children – putting a tennis ball underneath a handkerchief and pushing it along the floor pretending it had legs.

Not feeling so threatened now, and rather intrigued, Jackson followed the moving shirt, but as soon as he got closer to it the thing stopped and stayed still. So he retreated a few paces and then, as if sensing the coast was clear, the thing started moving again.

They had progressed in this manner for a few minutes before Jackson realised the bush was getting thicker now, plus he was well away from the road and he had lost sight of the car.

Then just as common sense started to kick in and he was deciding to go back, he heard a noise. Just a faint sound, like a little cry, or a whimper; hard to make out. He stayed still, silent, listening, and then watched, transfixed, as the shirt caught on a branch and then slowly slid off the creature's back.

Jackson held his breath and stared as a puppy emerged and turned round and stared at him, frozen with fear. Ready to run, untrusting, uncertain. It could have been no more than a few weeks old and was thin with black and white matted fur.

Jackson bent down, holding out his hand. Speaking gently, coaxing, wanting to take the fear from this small animal's eyes. Slowly, the puppy walked a few steps towards him, then stopped, hesitant, unsure, watching him.

Jackson moved fast then. In one quick movement, he stepped forward and scooped the animal up into his arms, cradling it. He stroked its head. He could feel the puppy shivering with fright and yet it made no attempt to escape.

So Jackson waited until he felt the animal relax a little bit before walking back to the car. He opened the door, holding tightly to the animal with one hand while he grabbed a towel from the back, and then laid it on the front seat and carefully put the puppy down. 'There you go,' he said. He found his bottle of water and poured some into the little recess between the seats. The puppy drank, then settled back onto the towel, turned around a few times and went to sleep.

Jackson started the car. He had a big smile on his face. Unbelievable, he thought. It was just by chance he had stopped next to that pile of garbage.

He could hear his wife's voice in his head. 'You should get another dog,' she had said. 'Keep you company on those long trips.'

He stroked the pup. 'Chance.' he murmured, 'that's what your name is, Chance.'

He glanced sideways and saw two floppy ears twitch.

The Tree House

It was late afternoon and Gerry slowed down the big four-wheel drive when he saw the track leading off to the left, away from the highway

'Why are we stopping, Dad?' Danny asked

'Well, I'm looking for somewhere to camp for the night.' He looked at his wife 'What do you reckon, Pat? Shall we give this a try?'

She nodded. 'Looks fine. Let's give it a go. We can always turn back if it doesn't lead anywhere.'

Gerry turned onto the track. It looked well used, with deep ruts indicating the passage of big vehicles. There had been tree felling in the area which was evident by some stumps here and there which had been left behind. He drove carefully for about a kilometre and was thinking about turning back as the track was beginning to peter out, and he was worried about having enough space to turn round if he needed to return to the highway. Plus thick foliage met overhead from trees either side, making a canopy which blocked out the sun, giving an eerie gloomy light, and Gerry was not feeling comfortable about continuing on.

Then he slowed down. A bright patch of sunlight had suddenly appeared up ahead shining onto a clearing, an absence of trees, unexpected and beautiful, like an oasis emerging from the gloom.

'Wow,' Danny exclaimed in delight. 'Look at that. Can we stop here, Dad?'

Gerry pulled up at the edge of the clearing and five-year-old Mandy was already undoing her seat belt.

'Hold on a minute. I'll get a bit closer.' Gerry drove on a little further and then braked. 'Okay,' he said. 'Everybody out and we'll have a look-see.'

It was a cleared patch of ground surrounded by trees, with tree stumps one to two feet high set in a circle around a shallow pit holding the old ashy remains of a fire. There were small white flowers, which looked a little like daises but with more petals, growing among stubby grass.

They all just stopped and stared slightly in awe for a few moments.

'It's a magic circle,' exclaimed Mandy in delight. 'Can we stay here, Dad?'

'Well, it sure looks like a great camping spot.' Gerry was slightly puzzled. 'I wonder why there are no signs. We wouldn't have known this was here if we hadn't found it by accident.'

'Maybe it's a secret place that not many people know about,' Pat suggested. 'I guess we just got lucky. It's a perfect spot.'

Danny was out of the car already with his soccer ball. The children had been allowed to bring toys. These occasional camping trips were Gerry's idea. 'To get the kids away from their tablets, the TV and computers. Out in the fresh air,' he had said. They also agreed not to use the phone unless absolutely necessary, although it must be said that Pat especially found it hard not to sneak a look now and again. But mostly it worked. Danny always brought his soccer ball. At ten years old, he was in the school junior football team and practised his dribbling skills whenever he could. Mandy had brought her Barbie doll with several changes of clothes.

'Okay, you two,' Gerry pointed to the children, 'we'll need some sticks to get a fire going and then we'll boil the billy and sort out something to eat. '

'Good, I'm starving.' Danny was already looking for sticks. 'Can we have sausages and beans?' He went over to the other side of the clearing. 'Come on, Mandy,' he called, 'you're supposed to be helping.'

It was the usual scenario. Pat getting the cooking utensils out, Gerry sorting out the two small tents, the kids off exploring and looking for wood chips.

Danny was soon back, arms full of bits of wood, Mandy with two or three sticks, and they plonked them down next to the fire pit, then scampered off again.

'Stay within sight,' Pat called.

They weren't gone for very long before coming back again.

'Guess what,' Danny shouted.

'What?' Gerry had one tent up. 'Come and help me with this tent, Danny.'

'We found a tree house.'

'Yes, a little fairy tree house.' Mandy sounded excited 'Come and see.'

'Okay.' Gerry wanted to get things done and everyone settled. 'After we've done setting up and had tea, then we'll have a look.'

'It's really cool, Dad. It's all carved. I think it's a Hobbit's house.' Danny had recently brought the book home from school and was into the world of Hobbits.

He had to curb his impatience, though, for the time being. A can of baked beans had been opened and sausages were sizzling in a pan over the fire. Then by the time the tents were up, tea was made and consumed and everything cleared away again, it was almost dark. Gerry figured that the sun had about twenty minutes before disappearing.

'So are you coming to see the tree house, Dad? Mum?' Danny was persistent now and anxious.

Gerry gave in and looked at Pat. 'Coming?' he asked her. 'We may as well go and check it out before it gets dark, or we won't get any peace.'

They knew their son. Once Danny got an idea in his head, he never let it go.

So they all went over to the other side of the clearing, and just a little way in under the trees, there it was, just as the children had said. A door had been carved into the trunk of an enormous tree. It was beautifully done and quite small and low to the ground. About two and a half feet wide and perhaps three feet high.

Gerry considered himself very knowledgeable when it came to wood carving and he exclaimed in admiration as he bent down and fingered the intricate design. 'This is excellent work,' he said. 'Who on earth could have done it? And why?' he added, sounding puzzled

'There's no door handle.' Mandy had been looking carefully. 'How can we get it open?'

'It's not a real door, sweetheart,' Pat told her. 'It's just a pretend one.'

'Oh,' she was disappointed. 'What's the good of a door if it doesn't open, then?'

Danny went round to the other side of the tree, hoping that there might have been a back door, but there was nothing. He returned to the front of the tree and put his weight on the door a couple of times, convinced it should open, much to the amusement of Gerry.

'Sorry, mate,' he said, 'afraid it's just a wood carving. Come on, you have to get settled in your tent before it gets too cold.'

Indeed, a breeze had sprung up and the sun had just about gone. So back they went to their tents. Sleeping bags, pillows, torches were dispensed, zips pulled up over flapping doors and eventually the children were tucked in. Gerry and Pat stayed by the fire and waited until they were sure the kids were settled and sleeping before turning in to their own tent They were all tired. When camping, the rule was to go to bed when it got dark and up with the sunrise and not to worry about the clock. At least, that was the plan.

Danny awoke during the night, needing the toilet, so he crept quietly outside using the torch and went behind a little bush alongside the tent. He was half asleep and eager to get back to his warm sleeping bag, so when he glanced sideways and saw a light coming from the direction of the tree house he didn't think too much of it. He guessed it was a reflection or light from the moon. It was a full moon tonight just rising over the tree tops.

If he hadn't been so eager to get back to bed and had gone to investigate, Danny might have realised that there really was a light coming from behind the little door which was half open. He might also have seen small beings emerging. Little people with long beards pointy hats, strange clothes and enormous feet. But unfortunately, he didn't see any of them.

Next morning, Gerry was up first, as usual, intending to get the fire going and the billy on to brew some tea. He frowned when he saw the neat pile of wood chips on the ground next to the fire pit. He didn't remember putting them there. Perhaps, he thought, Danny had, which was quite unlikely but possible, he supposed. He got the fire going anyway and waited for the rest of the family to get up. He turned to look as he heard Mandy give a squeal of delight. She was standing by her tent looking at the tree stump which she had been using as a table for her Barbie doll.

'Look, Dad,' she called when she saw him. 'A daisy chain!' She picked it up and went over to Gerry to show him. 'Mummy showed me how to make these, but I couldn't do it as good as this. There's another one too. It must be for Danny.'

Danny had by now emerged looking sleepy and he picked up the other daisy chain. He looked at it. There was no way he would wear a daisy chain, he thought. He imagined the reaction of his soccer playing mates. But then, unaccountably, he put it over his head. He looked around. Somehow it seemed the right thing to do in this special place, and he did a very unDanny-like thing and danced a little jig.

Mandy had puts hers on too and was dancing around with delight. 'It was the fairies,' she announced. 'The fairies made it for me.'

'Hobbits,' said Danny, 'definitely Hobbits.' He pretended to be joking, but later on that day when everyone was packing up ready to leave, and no one was paying him any attention, he went to check the little door again. It seemed to be just the same as yesterday, except for a pathway leading away from the door and many scuff marks in the dirt around the tree, and around the fireplace, and Danny knew.

His mother was calling him. 'Come along, Danny, get your bag, we're ready to go.'

'Hobbits,' he said to Mandy, as they settled themselves in the back of the car. 'It was definitely Hobbits.'

But she wasn't listening. Barbie was getting a change of clothes.

No-brainer

It was a fine day and Imelda had a clear view of the street below from her balcony. New World Apartments were thirty storeys high but she had opted for the sixth floor when she moved in; heights made her anxious. There were flats roofs on all of the buildings in this new age residential village and she could take the elevator when she had to go up there to collect groceries or anything else that might have been delivered by the helicopters. Every tenant had their own designated space; indeed, there was no need to go shopping any more. Everything was delivered.

It was getting towards dusk and soon the polidrones would be out looking for anyone loitering on the streets after curfew, which began at dusk, and then the people-scoopers would appear ready to capture illegals not quick enough to dodge their powerful beams of intense light. These unlucky people were never seen again. Anyone who managed to escape remained fugitives for the rest of their lives, or so Imelda had heard. She didn't know for sure and she wasn't likely to find out now. In fact, she had no reason to go out at all.

The new regime had come along with the new government who had promised to eradicate crime. It seemed to be working. People who had legitimate reasons for being out at night were issued with illuminated passes which they had to wear on their heads so that they could be seen by the polidrones. People in vehicles were generally left alone but spot checks were often done to catch drink or drug drivers.

The streets had been cleaned up as well. There was no litter to be seen. Litterers were heavily penalised, as were loiterers, speedsters, and pedestrians not using the correct crossings. All were spotted by the polidrones, who passed overhead with a low buzzling sound, swooping on malingerers. Larger prisons had been built to cope with the influx of miscreants. There were no long court cases any more. On the spot sentences were handed out, fines were issued or people were sent directly to prison depending on the seriousness of the crime which had been committed.

Imelda pondered on all of this as she sat and watched the people below as they hurried to their homes or hailed one of the automated driverless taxis, which had become the norm for some time now. She rose from her chair and went back into the main room, wedging herself with difficulty into the big armchair in front of the enormous television which covered almost all of the main wall of the lounge room.

She spoke loudly. 'Television on,' she said, and a beautiful blonde with blindingly white teeth appeared on the screen and responded with 'Good afternoon, Imelda. What programme would you like to watch? Your regular sitcom, or perhaps the news?'

Imelda gave a little jump as the voice spoke. She still wasn't used to someone talking to her out of the TV, but it was one of things which came with the apartment. She had spent just about every cent she had in the bank on moving here and still couldn't believe how lucky she had been. She had been on the waiting list for nearly a year and then someone had unexpectedly cancelled and she had been offered a year's lease, so she had quickly taken it. She had been here for three months now and absolutely loved her new life.

Everything was organised. She could do her writing in peace. She no longer had to go out to shop. She could talk to her friends in real time as though they were in the room with her. A hairdresser called when she needed one. A doctor appeared on the screen for consultation, and medication was delivered. There was a pool and gymnasium down on the ground floor, not that Imelda ever went there, but it was nice to know that it was there if she felt the need for exercise. The fact that since she had lived here she had never felt the need did bother Imelda a little bit sometimes, but she quickly dismissed the thought almost as soon as it crossed her mind.

She turned as she heard a sound from the small kitchenette. James had come to live with her a week ago. She had picked him out of the catalogue that advertised humanoid drones. 'Someone to do the housework and cook', she read. 'Pick out your preference.' There were several choices: an intellectual one, an athletic one, an old one, a young one, male or female and so on. Lots of choices, in fact. Imelda disliked doing housework, cooking was a chore; although, it must be said, she did like to eat and, as for the laundry, well, Imelda thought, why not get someone else to do that as well? She could afford it now. Her publisher had come up with lots of money and a promise of more if she could produce the next book within a certain deadline.

'All of our humanoids are domesticated', she had read, and you could have one on trial for a month before making a final decision. It was a no-brainer, she thought, and spoke into the phone chip embedded in her wrist. The number was answered straight away.

'How may I help you, Imelda?' a bright female voice asked.

Deciding she had nothing to lose and everything to gain, Imelda took the plunge. 'I'd like to try one of your humanoids,' she said. 'Are you sure they all do housework and cooking as well as the laundry?' she asked.

'Most certainly they do,' the voice replied. 'Have you decided which model you would like?'

'Well,' replied Imelda, 'I thought perhaps a butler-like person.'

'Yes, we have some very desirable butlers. Would you like young or old? Perhaps a young sexy one would suit you, Imelda. What do you think? You could always change over in a month if you're not happy and try something else.'

Imelda couldn't help smiling then. A young sexy humanoid? That'd be a bit of a laugh, she thought, but why not?

'Well, OK, I'll go with that. I'll give it a try,' she said.

'A sexy butler then, about forty years old, shall we say? About the same age as you, Imelda.'

That had thrown Imelda for a moment. How did this person know her age? 'Yes, that'd be fine,' she managed.

'You've made a good choice. I'll send the paperwork through and you can expect him the day after tomorrow.'

Imelda had waited impatiently for the call that the helicopter had a delivery for her and then finally it had come and she had made her way to the elevator which took her to the roof. She wondered what sort of a package her butler would come in, but to her surprise standing there waiting for her after the helicopter had disappeared was a handsome young man, dark hair, smart jacket, looking perfectly normal and carrying a suitcase.

He had spoken with a slight French accent as he held out his hand. 'How do you do, Imelda?'

'How do you do,' she responded, aware of how cold his hand felt. 'What is your name?' she asked him.

'James,' he said. 'I am James your butler,' and he gave her the most beautiful smile.

For a moment, Imelda forgot that he wasn't actually a human. Then, gathering herself together, she proceeded to walk back to the elevator. 'It's this way,' she said.

There were three bedrooms in her apartment and Imelda had prepared the second bedroom as well as she could for her butler's comfort, feeling a little anxious, not really knowing what a humanoid needed, but he was so pleased with his room and happy with the apartment, and so likeable, that she was feeling quite relaxed about it all now. She had showed him how everything worked, and he appeared to be so at home in the kitchen that he seemed like a member of her family already.

James had given her an envelope which contained a list of the duties he was programmed to perform: 'Your humanoid is programmed to cater for all your personal needs, as well as cooking, cleaning, washing, ironing, shopping. He does not use profanity, is even-tempered and also knows a few jokes.'

She had to laugh then. She had to keep that in mind for when she needed cheering up a bit.

Now James was hovering in the doorway. 'Dinner is ready, Imelda,' he said. 'I have made a chicken casserole. I hope you like it.'

She had prepared a list of foods she liked and disliked and James had proven himself to be a fantastic cook. In the past week, he had presented her with meals she would never have attempted to make herself. She turned the TV off again and made her way to the dining table, which was nicely set with wine glasses at the ready.

'Thank you, James.'

She was glad to see he was fully dressed. The first morning after his arrival, he had appeared at her bedroom door with a cup of tea and wearing just an apron wrapped around himself, no shirt, just beautiful bulging muscles, and then when he turned to go, she saw a pair of neat little buns peeping out from the opening at the back of his apron.

Imelda had kept her cool. 'Um, James, why are you not wearing any trousers?'

He smiled his gorgeous grin. 'I am a sexy butler,' he said. 'This is my uniform.'

'Well, that may be so, James,' Imelda was sounding a little prim,' but I prefer you to wear trousers. And a shirt,' she added.

'Very well, Imelda, as you wish,' he said, and since then had appeared fully dressed.

After that, they had settled into a comfortable routine. Imelda worked in the morning and then watched television, listened to music and talked to friends. Her house was spotless, laundry always up to date, and she had no reason to leave the apartment at all.

James spent a lot of time in his room when he wasn't working and she often wondered what he did in there. He never ate. She wondered if he slept. Sometimes he would sit and watch television and have a conversation with her about something he had seen or read about. He was very knowledgeable and it seemed as though everything he heard or saw was absorbed into his brain and kept for future reference. Imelda wanted to know how he operated. Did he have a battery, for instance, and if he did, how often it was charged up? But she didn't like to ask; perhaps she would when she knew him a little better. He could also play a good game of chess, Imelda discovered, and of course always won, but she didn't mind because she taught him to play Scrabble and she always beat him.

A few weeks later, it was Imelda's birthday and after dinner James surprised her with a birthday cake and candles in the shape of number 41. By this time, she had downed a few glasses of red, and when he appeared carrying the cake wearing his apron and nothing else, she didn't say a word. She thought he had an unusually smug expression on his face as he cut the cake and handed her a piece, and as he walked out of the dining room she stared at his rear for rather a long minute, before blinking a couple of times and then taking another large swig of wine.

As the days and weeks passed, Imelda finished her book, sent it off and had idea for the next one. She realised she would have to think about renewing her lease, or not, as the case might be. Could she give all this up and go back to live in the country where her parents had a farm where there was fresh air, fresh vegetables, exercise and a healthy lifestyle? She realised that she had not left her apartment since James had arrived. She sighed. It was a no-brainer really.

'I'm gonna need a bigger chair, she muttered.

James, in the kitchen, heard her and smiled.

Rocky

Mary Jane wanted a puppy. She begged and pleaded until her mum Rosie gave in, and when her daughter's tenth birthday came around, she said, 'Come on then, Mary Jane, let's go.'

'Go where?'

'You'll see,' Rosie said. 'It's a surprise.'

Mary Jane was used to her mum's surprises and she asked no more questions, but skipped out to the car, excitement cruising through her body like electric currents.

In the car she didn't ask any questions even though she was nearly bursting with curiosity. She watched out of the window wondering where they were going and when they stopped outside the pet shop she squealed, 'A puppy ! Am I going to get a puppy?'

Rosie smiled. 'Come on then. Out you get.'

It was a big pet shop; kittens, cats, puppies, dogs, snakes, tortoises, guinea pigs, hamsters and so on, and Mary Jane wandered around looking at everything. She stopped by the small enclosure where some cute puppies were sleeping in the corner. The sign at the front said, 'JACK RUSSELLS three months old' and she was about to say, 'Can I have one of those, Mum?' when a beautiful deep male voice from behind them said, 'Allo, darlin'.'

Mary Jane and Rosie both turned round at the same time and looked to see who had spoken, but there were no other customers nearby and the two staff members over at the counter were busily chatting.

'Allo, darlin',' said the voice again and then they looked up to see a large parrot perched in his cage, which was hanging on a hook attached to the ceiling. He was gorgeous, resplendent in his robe of bright red and green feathers. The cage looked as though it were home-made and there was a thick piece of wood at the bottom with the name Rocky carved into the side. His alert beady dark eyes were gazing at Mary Jane with such fixed intensity that she was mesmerised.

'Oh, he's beautiful,' she whispered in awe. She looked away for a moment at the puppies, then back to the parrot, her mind made up. She looked at her mum. 'Can I have the parrot instead of a puppy?' she asked.

Rosie pondered. She hadn't bargained on a parrot. But there again, she thought, a bird would probably be less work than a puppy, which would grow, which had to be walked, poop to be cleaned up, bathed and brushed and so on. Whereas a bird would just need its cage cleaned, and to be fed and watered. So she nodded. 'Well, if you're sure, Mary Jane. You'll have to clean the cage, you know. It'll be your responsibility.'

'I will, I promise.' Mary threw her arms around her mum. Thank you. This is the best birthday present ever.'

So that was that, the deal was done. Rosie was pleased that the bird and its cage turned out to be much cheaper than a Jack Russell puppy would have been. They put Rocky on the back seat of the car and Mary Jane sat beside him to keep the cage steady.

Rocky was quiet all the way. He just sat on his perch and gazed at Mary Jane, who was completely entranced and couldn't wait to get him home. She was busy thinking about things she could teach him to say.

They put the parrot on the bench in the kitchen and gave him some water and bird seed which they had been given at the pet shop. For a brief moment, Rosie wondered why the owner seemed so happy to sell the parrot to them; she had thought that a talking parrot would have been quite a drawcard in a pet shop.

Mary Jane's dad Dave was a big burly bloke who worked at the docks and when he came home from work later that afternoon, he shouted out his usual greeting, 'I'm home!' looking for his daughter, who always ran to greet him with a hug. Today, however, there was no sign of her, until she appeared suddenly, calling out to him.

She grabbed hold of his hand and pulled him into the kitchen. 'See what Mum bought me for my birthday,' she said.

Dave spun round as a lovely male voice said, 'Allo, darlin'.'

'Who the…what the…' Dave tried not to use expletives in the house, but this time he sure came close. He peered into the cage, and then watched, fascinated as Rocky ruffled his feathers and began preening himself and jumping up and down on his perch with excitement. Then leaning forward as close to the edge of the cage as he could, he fixed a bright alert eye with such intensity on Dave that he stepped back, shaking his head in disbelief as Rocky said, 'Allo, darlin'', in a voice not so raucous as before and, though Dave could scarcely believe it, sounding quite sexy.

He recoiled in horror. 'What the f…' He nearly lost it this time and turned away, stalking out of the room calling his wife. 'Rosie! Rosie!'

She came running. 'What is it, Dave? What's wrong? Are you OK?'

'That bird,' he spluttered. 'What happened to the puppy, then? I thought she wanted a puppy.'

'Well, she changed her mind.' Rosie glanced up at her husband. 'Don't worry, dear. Mary Jane is going to look after it and teach Rocky some new words.'

'Well, I hope so,' Dave muttered, somewhat appeased, 'and it had better go outside on the veranda. I'm not having it in the house.'

Mary Jane complained a bit about her parrot being relegated to the outside, but the days were warm, and at night time a cover could be thrown over the cage, which sat on an old picnic table.

So for a while this all worked very nicely. Every day after school Mary Jane would hurry home, give Rocky food and water and clean out the cage. The parrot seemed to be quite tame and sat on Mary Jane's shoulder, making no attempt to fly away,

She tried hard to teach him to say something else but without much success. Although one day when she was late home from school having started dance classes, an after-school activity which was Mary Jane's latest passion, he didn't give his usual greeting to her of 'Allo, darlin'.' In fact, he was sounding very cross, and with a baleful eye regarding her intently, he called out 'Wheresthecracker?' Mary Jane was a little freaked out and rushed inside to tell her mum and to come and listen, but he wouldn't say it again, especially after having been fed.

One day Dave brought a workmate home and they decided to go out to the backyard with a couple of beers for a chat, when the very sexy-sounding 'Allo darlin'' rang out loud and clear, as it usually did whenever Dave went out into the backyard.

Dave's mate Joe was a bit of a wag and after watching Rocky fixing his bright eyes on Dave and watching his every move, Joe said, 'I think that parrot's in love with you, mate!' and Dave nearly lost it again.

'Bloody bird,' he muttered.

A few days later, Rosie had a phone call from the manager of the pet shop. He was sounding very nervous, and was apologetic. 'I'm so sorry,' he said, 'but I have a gentleman in the shop who is enquiring after his parrot ,which was apparently stolen from him some weeks ago. He's…um…an entertainer in a cabaret show and it seems the bird disappeared from his dressing room when he was away on tour. His name is Peter,' he added.

This was a bit of a bombshell, thought Rosie. 'Does he know the parrot's name?' she asked

'Yes, he said it's Rocky. I'm so sorry,' he repeated. 'But the gentleman asks if he can come and see you to identify it. If it turns out that he is the owner, it will of course be up to you what to do, as it's now your property, but I must stress that I had no idea it was stolen when I bought it from the other gentleman who sold it to me. I will of course refund you in full if you decide to return the parrot to its owner. That's if this gentleman turns out to be the owner.' He waited for Rosie to say something.

She didn't have much of a choice, she thought, did she? So 'Yes,' she said, 'all right. You can send him round. You have my address.'

While she waited, Rosie went out to see Rocky, and he gave her the usual greeting. His cage was clean and neat, water bowl full, which she had seen to herself today, because Mary Jane had her dancing lessons after school on Fridays and then had to be reminded to attend to her pet. This had been happening a lot lately and Rosie wasn't too surprised; she suspected the novelty of owning a parrot was wearing off.

When the knock came on the door, she had decided what she was going to do, She gazed up at the tall young man standing on the doorstep, who had an anxious look on his face. His eyeshadow was colourful, as were his fingernails, and his blond hair was to his shoulders.

He held out his hand. 'How do you do, Mrs Blackmoor. I'm Peter. I'm so sorry to bother you but I've been worried sick about Rocky and when my friend told me he thought he had seen him in that pet shop, I came as quickly as I could. I've been interstate and I've only just come back.'

Rosie, slightly bemused, shook his hand. He seemed genuine, she thought, but Rocky would know. 'Come on through,' she said. 'He's out the back.'

As soon as Rocky spotted Peter, he went berserk, banging himself against the side of the cage and calling out 'Allo darlin'' over and over. Peter rushed over and opened the cage door. The parrot flew out, landed on his shoulder and began rubbing himself against the young man's face.

'Hello, darling,' said Peter. 'I've found you.' His eyes filled with tears, and so did Rosie's.

'Come inside and have a coffee,' she said.

So he did, with Rocky still perched lovingly on his shoulder. They had a nice chat, dispelling any doubts Rosie might have had about Peter's ownership. He didn't stay long, there was a show to get back to, and when he left, Rosie helped him deposit Rocky, who was back in his cage, safely in the passenger seat of his car.

Dave and Mary Jane both arrived home together that afternoon, Dave having picked her up from school. Rosie told them what had happened, and that Rocky had gone back to his original owner.

'I didn't get to say goodbye.' Mary Jane was a little upset. But not as upset as one would have expected her to be at the loss of her pet.

As for Dave, when he went out into the backyard later on, it was strangely quiet. Not that he would have admitted it to anyone, he could barely admit it to himself, but he missed that bloody bird.

Heatwave

For the fourth time that day, a wave of heat engulfed Sarah's face and neck like a blast from a furnace. She dabbed at her hot sweaty face with a sodden handkerchief and looked around the room to see if anyone was watching. But no one seemed to have taken any notice of her discomfort, except her husband, who had happened to glance at her standing beside him while he was engaged in conversation with the senior partner and his gorgeous wife. But Sarah had caught the swift look of disgust on his face. She made an excuse and turned away.

'It's important that we're both there on Friday night,' he had told her. 'It's the last event for the year. If I want to be considered for promotion, then I have to attend these functions. And you have to be seen to be supporting me.' He had peered closely at her face. 'What's wrong with you anyway? It's not that hot. Why are you looking like a beetroot?'

She had explained it to him. 'It's a hot flush. There's nothing I can do about it. They just come and go.'

'Well, go and see the doctor,' he said. 'Get some pills or something. Whatever it takes. Just get yourself fixed up. Wear some make-up or something. It's embarrassing.' He had stalked off muttering about women and their silly complaints.

So she had been to the doctor. He had prescribed some stuff which apparently wasn't working. She had applied make-up which just looked disgusting and patchy when she perspired as she was doing now.

Sarah headed for the women's rest room hoping no one would notice her absence. She hated these formal functions. She hated having to keep up appearances just so that her husband could display her by his side like an attractive appendage.

She couldn't cope with the polite inane chitchat and the people with whom she had nothing in common. She didn't enjoy watching women trying to outdo one another with their designer clothes, and the carefully veiled catty remarks, said with deceptive smiles on their Botoxed faces. She couldn't stand the fake bonhomie of men trying to impress other men to gain favour, to get ahead in the business.

Sarah looked at her face in the mirror and got her make-up out of her bag to try and repair the smudgy look of the mascara. When the door suddenly opened, she gave a little jump, but thankfully it was only the cleaning lady.

'Don't mind me,' said the friendly-looking soul carrying toilet paper and a mop. 'Just checking everything's OK.' She peered at Sarah in the mirror, and smiled knowingly. 'Having a hot flush, are you, luv? It's a bugger, isn't it?' She passed through into one of the toilets.

'Yes,' replied Sarah, 'it's a bugger.' She paused in thought for a long moment.

Suddenly she made a decision. Grabbing a bunch of paper towels, she doused them in soap and water and began scrubbing her face. She carefully wiped away every bit of make-up and kept going until every scrap of it was gone. Her face looked, clean, bright, fresh and shiny. She smiled at her reflection.

The cleaning lady finished her jobs and on her way out looked at Sarah in the mirror again. She gave her a wink. 'You look ten years younger, luv.'

Sarah put her make-up back in her bag, found her comb, unpinned the carefully coiffured hairstyle which had taken her ages to perfect, and dropped into the waste bin the hair extensions which had been woven into the topknot. She combed her hair out until it was flowing around her shoulders. Then she took off her uncomfortable high-heeled shoes, and wriggled her toes with a happy sigh.

Sarah opened the restroom door and cautiously peered out. There was no one in sight. With her bag in one hand and shoes in the other, she padded barefoot along the passage leading to the front door. An attendant was there and he opened it, giving her a curious look and then a polite smile as he ushered her out.

'Good evening, madam,' he said, 'and have a Happy Christmas.'

'Thank you,' replied Sarah, giving him a smile. 'You too.'

The sun was setting, making a beautiful sky as she stepped out into the evening feeling a little panicky, and she glanced back into the building for a moment, but there was no one following her. She waved down a passing taxi.

The driver greeted her. 'Where to, miss?'

Sarah realised she would have to make a plan. She gave him her address. She would have to make a quick stop to change out of this dress into something comfortable and get some other shoes on. Then who knows where? It didn't matter.

As she settled into the cool comfort of the taxi, Sarah let out a big sigh of relief. She felt the tension drain from her body and then came the tears. She knew there would be repercussions, but it didn't matter any more. She felt liberated, free. She had all the time in the world to decide what to do next.

Sarah realised the driver had spoken to her. He had the weather forecast on the radio and had remarked that it looked as though they would be having another heatwave.

'Yes, said Sarah. 'It's a bugger, isn't it?'

Puzzled dark eyes looked at her through the rear-vision mirror and she started to laugh.